YOUNG EAGLE RISING

YOUNG EAGLE RISING

ELLIE JOYCE

The Book Guild Ltd

First published in Great Britain in 2022 by
The Book Guild Ltd
Unit E2 Airfield Business Park,
Harrison Road, Market Harborough,
Leicestershire. LE16 7UL
Tel: 0116 2792299
www.bookguild.co.uk
Email: info@bookguild.co.uk
Twitter: @bookguild

This work is entirely fictitious and bears no resemblance to any persons living or dead.

Typeset in 11pt Adobe Jenson Pro

Printed and bound in the UK by TJ Books LTD, Padstow, Cornwall

ISBN 978 1915122 957

British Library Cataloguing in Publication Data.
A catalogue record for this book is available from the British Library.

For my grandmother,
who introduced me to wrestling and vowed
her teeth had been pulled out by gypsies.

FAREWELL TO IRELAND

I hoped the ship had already sailed. Nothing would have pleased me more than the sight of that wooden hulk sweeping through the waves of Lough Foyle without me. I didn't want to leave my friends, and I definitely didn't want to sail thousands of miles across an ocean to the New World. 'I won't go!' I shouted defiantly, but no one listens to a thirteen-year-old.

The day I'd been dreading finally arrived – a clear May morning in the year 1735. I sat in the cart and sulked as we rumbled along the dirt road from Newtown-Limavady toward Londonderry docks. Da, stony-faced at the reins, whipped the old cob to pick up the pace or we'd never arrive at the quay in time. He was a small man, stocky; good with his fists. In his younger days, he'd been a boxer and made a good name for himself because he fought without wrappings on his knuckles and levelled many a man twice his size. In the evening I would sit at his feet by the fire, leaning against his knees, sucking in the smell of baccy, whisky and wood smoke that hung about his clothes. I would have known him in the darkest night from that scent alone.

That morning he was wearing his Sunday belt even though it wasn't Sunday. Woven from strands of plaited leather it was finished with a large, shiny buckle. I'd often fingered the creased ridges, breathed in the scent of the soft, worn leather and thought of the hands that had worked such a fine piece. Da usually held his trousers up with string, but today being a special occasion, he'd strapped the belt around his waist and announced with a wink, 'If yer going to drown, boy – then drown in yer best!'

Drown? That was comforting. I looked down at the solid ground beneath the cart wheels and shivered.

Ma sat beside him sniffing up her sorrow, ten-month-old Thomas bundled in a shawl on her lap, and her old woollen dress tucked under her thighs to keep out the cold. She'd cut her lovely, long, chestnut locks to help pay for passage – hair for wig making fetched a handsome price – and ever since the shearing clippers had severed her curls, she'd worn a bonnet to hide her short, stubby tufts. Her looks weren't helped by the wide, pink scar across her chin where she'd fallen over the doorstep as a child. When her skin shrank pale with cold, that scar sat like a thick, pink worm beneath her lips.

But while she was no beauty, she was brave. In her younger days, she'd worked in a fine house for wealthy folk, and when she married, they gave her a little silver jug as a wedding present. Da wanted to sell it to help pay for passage, but she defied him, not a common occurrence in our house, and saved her precious little jug from being sold. 'Take yer thieving hands off it, John! I'm not selling it!' Folding her arms, she tapped her foot and glared at Da, who finally surrendered, and Ma got to keep her little treasure.

Lizzy lay asleep beside me, her toss of dark, knotted hair like a rat's nest on my knees. Wearing a brown linen dress, woollen jacket, black woollen stockings and worn boots, she curled up tightly against the fresh morning air. At eight years of age, she understood nothing except we were leaving home. I can't say I understood much more myself, but that was my fault. I didn't want to understand.

My brother Bacon-face sat opposite me hugging his knees against the cold, the collar of his jacket pulled high around his ears. His given name was James, but I called him Bacon-face because at eleven years old he was a ruddy, round-faced lad who looked like a boiled ham. Sturdy and thickset like Da, he was a born fighter with a punch like a blacksmith. Unfortunately, during one of his many brawls about the village, he'd been pinned down by his long hair, which made him more than a little angry. So, seeing Ma's success with the clippers, he had cut his own curly locks, eagerly chopping without a looking glass. His remaining hair now resembled a pile of dark, dry cat sick, and woe to anyone who gave even the slightest snigger.

Aunt Sarah sat on the other side of Da. She had come to bid us farewell and return the cart to Limavady. She always said the good Lord had put her together when He needed His Sunday rest because her poor back was that bent she walked with a stick; the smooth, worn top rubbed shiny-black from years of her greasy fingers. Her hair was thick as a thatch. I could have sheltered under it in a storm. She also had a bockety left eye with a will of its own, no matter where the right eye was looking, that left eye was staring somewhere else. I loved her dearly but was dreading her final embrace because the rotten stench of her breath made my eyes water. She could take the rust off a bucket at twenty paces. When she came close, I would take a deep breath and hold it until I was bursting, hoping she would finish with the talk before I turned blue and hit the ground.

At our feet jangled a heap of bulging hemp sacks filled with chisels, hammers, hand saws, axe heads, a shovel, bags of seeds, old blankets, a few bowls and pots and remedies Ma had prepared for all manner of sickness. Da had entrusted the weapons to me; two shot flasks, two powder horns and a pair of fowling guns, each almost six feet in length, which made them a good bit bigger than me because, unlike my brother, I was a skinny wee runt of a lad.

Bacon-face was weighed down by metal-jawed rabbit traps and a long, two-man saw wrapped in thick linen. The final item was a large, rolled, tarred canvas to shield ourselves against the weather until we had a home in the 'better life'.

I had already said farewell to the grandma I adored. To earn her keep, she spun flax, then dyed the finished yarn with yellow meadowsweet, marsh marigold and petals of golden gorse. Over the years, the perfume had gradually soaked into her skin. That morning I laid my head on her shoulder and breathed in her fragrance until it hit the pit of my lungs, wishing I could bottle that smell and carry it with me. But there was more to Grandma than spinning flax. She had what Ma called 'the gift'; she had visions, heard voices, and occasionally, on a good day, brought messages from the dead. I often thought the spirit world must be a very crowded place.

'Don't you go telling no one, William,' Ma wagged the finger, 'Gran's gift is a secret. The Church doesn't look kindly on people who talk to the dead! If you were to tell, she would be tied to a stake with flames licking her heels before the last word had left yer lips!'

So, from an early age, I knew we had a witch in the house. My witch. I loved her wizened face and twinkling black eyes. I loved the bony bumps on the joints of her gnarled fingers. I even loved her black, crooked teeth, never quite certain if they were about to fall down her throat or grip a while longer to her gums.

Every so often it fell to me to shave her spiky chin. She would snap out the old cut-throat razor then wag the finger at me to be attentive to the task. Once, in too much haste, I accidentally sliced off her hairy mole. Her chin bled for days. I thought she was going to die. My punishment was to sleep with that bloody, black lump under my head for a week. I would wake with it stuck to my cheek, but I was a lot more careful with the cut-throat after that.

If I was felled with fever, it was Grandma who sat with me, and she was never short of surprises. Once, when I was on the mend from a bout of *the squirts*, she waited until everyone was working in the fields, then beamed, 'A bit of collar-and-elbow is what you need, lad.'

'Collar-and-elbow, Gran?'

But she was already tugging my long, chaotic, chestnut locks with her old, bone comb. My hair hadn't seen a comb for months, and I doubted this particular one was up to the task as it had even less teeth than Grandma. I winced and squealed in protest as she pulled at the knots, but she would have none of it. 'Hush yer screeching or I'll take the clippers to it, and then you'll look like yer brother!'

That was threat enough; I kept my gob firmly shut. Satisfied at last I looked more respectable, we climbed up onto the cart where again I asked, 'Grandma, what *is* collar-and-elbow?'

She gave the old cob a whip and the wheels began to roll. 'The wrestling, boy! We're away to watch the wrestling at Artikelly!'

We jiggled along country lanes where pale, yellow primroses peeped from under hedges of wild hazel and white hawthorn blossom drifted like snow. The nearer we came to Artikelly, the busier the lanes became, crowded with men of all ages walking toward the village. Many raised a hand in acknowledgement as we passed and Grandma pulled to a halt to let old George, the saddler from Limavady, hop on the cart to spare his bandy legs. Before long, we veered from the lane and followed a short track to a large stone barn. Climbing down, Grandma tethered the cob to a gate post, then we joined the excited crowd, paying our halfpenny fee to get through the door with all the rest.

Inside the barn was bigger than I'd expected. I had never seen so many people in one place, not even in church. Barefoot wrestlers prowled around, eyeing the competition and limbering their muscles. Everyone was buzzing with talk of who would win; the parish champion or a chancer who might have to be carried home. The air was thick with the smell of sweat and beer, and speech was loud and blunt, I heard words I wasn't allowed to repeat at home. This was not a place for ladies. In truth, Grandma was the only woman allowed past the door and seemed rightly respected. Burly men doffed their caps, even buying her a drink, a dram of whisky appeared and she downed the lot in one gulp. There wasn't a soul present who hadn't used the services of my grandma, being a wise woman had its advantages. That day, she wagered a farthing, then wagged the finger again – I was to say nothing to Ma – *ever*. Betting was the devil's game.

Now, when I entered that barn, I knew nothing about the art of collar-and-elbow, but I soon learned. The contestants grabbed the collar and elbow of their opponent, grunting and grappling and sparring with their legs and feet – each trying to bring the other man down. I was soon cheering and clapping with the thrill of each match and screeching, 'flat-back-fall!' or, 'flying-mare!', which was a throw that could break a man's back if he didn't land well. Money changed hands as wrestlers were praised or limped away to bind their injured limbs. I loved every moment of it.

Grandma, meanwhile, was happy as a pig in mud because she won a few coppers and bought the best hot potatoes I have ever tasted; their skins black and crispy from the fire and the inside dripping in butter. It was a grand day.

She coughed all the way home. As far back as I could remember, she had suffered from tar-lung and breathed like an overworked horse, but she had always been kind to me and I loved her for it. Wrapped in the blanket, I leaned against her shoulder, a sudden fear rolling over me. 'Ma's going to take yer head off for this, Grandma.'

Her eyes flashed with mischief. She could mimic the voice of my ma so well it sent shivers down my spine, '*John! That mother of yer's took the lad to the wrestling! She's teaching him bad ways!'* Passing the reins into one hand, she put an arm around my shoulders and held me close. 'Don't you fret, boy. You leave yer ma to me.'

I never forgot that day with Grandma. Of all the folk we were leaving behind, I would miss her most of all. From the day she first gathered me in her arms, there had been a special bond between us and I blamed my parents for breaking it. I had yet to learn that no amount of distance can break the tie between a witch and her grandchild.

I prayed we'd lose a wheel on the way to the docks and that would be the end of our travels; we'd fail to arrive on time and have to return home. Unfortunately, the wheels held, and we climbed down from the cart to see a multitude of people sobbing and wailing along the quayside with enough tears to raise the sea level. Ma cringed and pulled her bonnet lower over her stumpy hair. She needn't have worried. Some folk had sold their teeth and they looked much worse.

Wearing the only clothes I possessed – breeches, linen shirt, woollen jacket and a pair of Da's old boots – I huddled against the wall and gazed up at a ship larger than I could ever have imagined. The *Mary* sat like a huge sea monster waiting to gobble us into its belly. It dwarfed the fishing boats bobbing in the harbour. A web of thick, black rope hung above the wooden deck and stretched so far up the mast I had to shade my eyes against the morning sun to get a glimpse of the top. Barefoot sailors wearing neckerchiefs, canvas shirts, knitted caps, and with knives in lanyards hanging from their baggy breeches, were loading barrels, goats, chickens in wicker crates, buckets, candles and firewood, while others scuttled aloft where the sails lay furled like the hem of a fine lady's gown.

Bacon-face pointed to the barrels. 'I hope there's mutton in them there casks,' he mumbled. He was hungry. We were all hungry.

Every passenger on that quay was gaunt-faced and grey. Some had small parcels of food thrust into their hands by kin who looked half-starved themselves. Others carried all manner of things; spinning wheels, tables, chairs, baskets, fishing nets, crates and kegs, while some poor souls had nothing but the clothes on their backs.

'William – hold Lizzy's hand!' ordered Ma. She wagged the finger at me. The women in my family were born wagging the finger. I gazed down at Lizzy's fearful blue eyes and drew her in against my shirt, sweeping an arm around her shoulders to reassure her, when in all honesty, I was afeared we'd be blown to rags by a storm or caught in the jaws of a mighty fish and sink without a trace.

We were finally called aboard. With Lizzy clinging to my arm, I reluctantly crossed the gangplank and clambered into the bowels of the beast to find Bacon-face guarding a space below decks as though the boards were made of gold. This was where we would eat and sleep, surrounded by our possessions. I passed the fowling guns to him and he perched himself on our belongings like a king ready to defend his crown. If anyone tried to take even one inch of our space they would face the wrath of my brother, which would mean a fight before we even left the dock.

Leaving Lizzy with him, I joined my parents on the top deck where Ma was almost fainting with grief. Even hardy men were wringing their hands and wiping away tears. Shouts from the shore met with desperate cries from the ship as people called a final farewell to folk they loved. I had never seen my ma so distraught, her arms stretching toward a sister she would never again see in this life. I hadn't realised our departure would be so gut-wrenching. In truth, I hadn't thought that far ahead. Wallowing in my own misery, I'd done nothing but complain for weeks. I had sulked and argued over every little thing and made everyone's life miserable without any consideration for my folks who struggled daily to pay the high rent and work land they didn't own, or were ever likely to own.

Sheer desperation had forced them to make this treacherous voyage across the sea. I was suddenly ashamed of my behaviour. I could be a selfish, sullen wee brat at times, vexing the whole company.

Da wrapped his arms tightly around Ma's shoulders, holding her steady.

'Come now, my darlin' girl,' he whispered, 'think on all our plans! We will have our own land and be servants to none! With God's good grace there will be better days ahead. Wipe yer eyes now and don't be fretting. One day I'll buy you silk stockings and a fine feathered hat and you'll be the queen of the New World.' A small smile grew on her lips like a wild rose opening its petals.

'Stand by to set sail!' called the ship's master. My guts were suddenly filled with nervous, tickly ants as the gangplank was pulled away and ten yards of water yawned between me and Ireland. It may as well have been a hundred miles. There was no going back.

THE JOURNEY

'Lay aloft and loose all sails!'

The ship slowly rode the calm waters of the Foyle estuary toward the sea; the old planks groaning and griping as though they too were complaining about leaving Ireland. Passing the rocky point of Malin Head, the wide Atlantic suddenly lay before us, sparkling in the sunlight.

'Let fall!' called the master. High above the deck, huge sails dropped, billowing like petticoats. 'Set your lower topsails! Haul away your sheets! Set your upper topsails!'

The sails stretched tight, cracking like wet linen in the breeze, and the change in pace was instant. Like a horse that loves to run, that ship began to race through the white-tipped waves. Salty spray drizzled my face and stung my lips. The briny smell of seaweed tickled my nose. Wind battled my hair. It smacked the sails and rattled the pulleys as a host of seabirds followed the churning, turquoise wake behind the ship. I'd never been on a boat in my life. It was thrilling!

Leaving behind the shelter of the land, the ship began to pitch and yaw and folk began to retch, learning the hard way not to spew into the wind. As it happened, we were good sailors, apart from Ma, who was gooseberry green. She refused all food for the first two days, perhaps with good reason because Da called it pup mutton and said it was dog.

As the weeks passed, the sailors instructed all us lads in the workings of that ship. I learned with great diligence, but swiftly decided I had no desire to be a sailor; water of such a depth scares me witless. We even learned how to tie knots; a reef knot, a bowline knot and an anchor hitch, and in the evening, when the oil lanterns swung fore and aft and our little ship was but a pinhead of light in that vast, dark ocean, we played dice and cards, our laughter echoing far across the lonely, lapping waves.

There was one old sailor who fascinated me above the rest – Scuttle-Butt Bill. Baccy-stained teeth ringed his gums like a harbour wall and he spat like a bonfire, but he kept us highly entertained with stories of pirates, monsters of the deep and the horrors of a sea called the Sargasso. He frightened Bacon-face more than I could have done with a month's planning. I believe that's why I liked him so much.

'See wur a shark damn near ate me alive!' He held up a pink, crinkle-scarred hand. 'But ol' Scuttle-Butt 'ad the better of 'im!' He lowered his voice and we all leaned in close. 'Don't never desire to sail in the Sargasso! In yon thick seaweed, a ship can struggle like a fly in a web, its fate already sealed. Ships are caught in them calm waters 'til sailors run mad wi' thirst or throw thursels o'erboard – the scorchin' sun hoverin' above 'til naught remains but the bleached bones o' the dead! Many a ghost ship 'as drifted thur for years 'til water seeps through the shrinkin', shrivellin' beams an' drags the ship slowly down to the depths an' the monsters that lurk below the waves!'

Bacon-face barely closed his eyes for two nights after hearing those tales.

11

Although rations were meagre, the weeks passed with no great hardship until July, when to our dismay the barrels of drinking water turned rancid in the heat and I learned thirst was worse than hunger. We lay below decks trying to keep out of the sun, but in that cramped gloom the heat became stifling and the place stank like a pigsty. Desperate for fresh air, I wearily climbed the steps and sank onto the deck in the shade of the mizzen mast. If we had but one more week of these conditions, we wouldn't live to see Philadelphia.

Now, I had worked in the fields since I could stay upright and knew the signs of foul weather; the change in the smell of the air and the rising wind and men running for huge sheets to tie down the hayricks. But this was no grassy field. A sudden wind punched the sails. The ship lurched. Scrambling to my feet, I grabbed a rope and held on with all my might as the black sea began to churn and mountainous clouds, fat with fury, wrapped the ship in an eerie green shadow.

Captain Liston, strutting the deck in his black tailcoat and broad-brimmed hat, called, 'Mister Boatswain, prepare to heave to!'

'Comin' about to heave to, Cap'in!' cried the boatswain. 'Headsail backed to windward, lads! Mainsail to leeward! Step lively there!'

The ship suddenly slowed and turned through the wind as heavy drops of water smacked my face and dotted the deck. I licked my dry, cracked lips. This was no salty sea spray – it was rain! The good Lord himself must have squeezed the clouds through a mangle because a flood suddenly lashed the sails and sent tumbling waterfalls splashing over the deck. I flung wide my arms, threw back my head, opened my mouth and lapped those silver drops until a cool river of fresh, sweet rain ran down my parched throat. Shrieking with joy, passengers spilled from the deck hatch carrying bowls, mugs and even piss pots, holding them beneath the dripping sails until they overflowed with bubbling, frothy water.

Da came running toward me, slip-sliding on the wet planks. 'Below decks, William! Make haste! Captain's orders!'

Like rats diving down a hole, we scrambled back down the steps into the dim light, steadying ourselves against beams and clinging to our possessions as waves crashed over the ship in raging, foaming torrents, seeping down through the planks until our clothes were drenched and we shivered with cold. For two long days and nights, we listened to the wailing of the wind and the screams of folk hurled through the gloom by each surge and roll of the ship. The water ran red around our ankles from splintered bones, bloody gashes and all manner of injuries. Yet the danger crept past us all, except one – young Bonnie McKay.

I had become acquainted with a young labourer from Ballintoy named Edward McKay. Although he had no schooling, he knew all about the stars, and on clear nights, we'd gaze heavenward toward the sparkling sky. His da had been a sailor and taught him to navigate by those twinkling lights, so Edward taught me how to find the seven points of the plough and the bright North Star. He believed the earth moved around the sun. What a notion!

Now Edward had no living wife, but he did have a blonde, curly-haired three-year-old angel named Bonnie. During that storm, she slipped from her da's dripping arms and slammed head first into a side beam. She was dead in a blink. The howls of that poor man were harrowing. He hugged her lifeless body for days, refusing to release her until two kind women gently prized the child from his arms. From that moment, he spoke not a single word. The little girl was weighted, stitched in a blanket, and lowered over the side with barely a splash. I think that good man lost all reason after the tragedy because he took no nourishment or drink from that moment, and several days later, despite our desperate search, we realised he was no longer aboard ship.

'Land ahoy!'

After almost three months at sea, we finally spied land! Rushing to the bow, we peered through the morning sea mist with such cheering it was a wonder they didn't hear us back in Ireland! The *Mary* sailed around a point of land the sailors called Cape Island, then crept up a narrowing river. Soon, we could see settlements along the banks, their chimneys puffing grey, curling smoke into the cold air. I wondered what life was like beyond those small villages. Was it as wild as I feared?

A pilot boat approached to guide us through the shallows and I noticed the sailors paying particular attention as it drew close. 'Wur watchin' for pirates, lad,' Scuttle-Butt muttered. 'They take o'er the pilot boats, then climb aboard the ship an' steal everythin' they can carry! This town wus once the greatest refuge for pirates on the whole east coast!'

Fortunately for us, the pilot wasn't a pirate and guided us safely toward our destination. We passed the mouth of a narrow river Scuttle-Butt called the Skokihl, then without warning, Philadelphia loomed out of the morning mist. What a wonderful sight! So much colour after the grey ocean! So many tall buildings! Elbowing my way to the prow, I stood there, mesmerised by my first real view of the town.

The quayside was humming with traders and merchants bargaining for barrels of silver-scaled fish. Women in bright bonnets were selling wriggling eels. Gulls were fighting over dead crabs and fish heads, swooping and fluttering like puppets on strings. Sailors hugged sweethearts they hadn't seen for many a long month. The whole place smelled of brine and seaweed and – I sniffed – fresh bread? Somewhere nearby there must be a baker's shop. I was so hungry I thought I would pass into glory for want of those warm loaves!

A voice at my shoulder made me start, 'Is Philadelphia to yur likin'?' asked Scuttle-Butt with a crooked smile.

'I hardly know!' I cried, 'I never thought to see so many ships! Are they all from Ireland?'

'No, lad!' he cackled. 'Look at thur ensigns. They's from Barbados, Jamaiky an' France, an' some bearin' Palatines an' Dutch! I've seen them all a'fore!'

'You know this port, Scuttle-Butt?'

'Indeed I do, young man, an' I like it better each time I come! Look, way o'er thur!' He pointed further along the waterfront to where the skeleton of a new ship sat as high as the eaves of the nearby buildings. 'Thur's the ol' West ship-buildin' yard! Thur's a ropewalk jus' beyon' it, an' that two-story brick buildin' beside the ramp is the Penny Pot Tavern – a favourite wi' all us sailors 'cause it sells beer for a penny a pot! An' that street thur,' he continued, giving a broad sweep of his arm toward the buildings beyond the wharf, 'is Front Street, wur you'll find the Quaker meetin' house an' the courthouse, which 'as a balcony, an' sometimes you can 'ear them callin' out the proclamations from 'ere!'

I could barely take it all in. My gaze drifted to another landing where men, black as tar, their backs bent under large hemp sacks, were unloading cargo. There seemed but one punishment if they stumbled; a lash from a whip. Scuttle-Butt must have seen the alarm on my face because he leaned over and whispered, 'They's slaves, boy. Whole country makin' money off the backs o' them men.'

His words didn't sit lightly with me, but there was so much to see I couldn't turn my mind to anything except the noise and bustle of the harbour. I dearly wanted to see all the diversions of the town, but we weren't here to see the sights. There would be no time for dawdling. When we finally touched solid ground, we would need to go in search of a horse, cart and provisions.

As the *Mary* slid alongside a landing stage, heaving lines were thrown ashore and looped over large, iron dock cleats, but it still took half the day to disembark because the master had to state under oath to the Collector of Duties that we were God-fearing folk of sound character. Some people were obliged to stay aboard because they were diseased, or hadn't paid for the journey so became servants to pay the debt, but we stumbled ashore with only one thought – where to find food. Da had been told our coins were acceptable for trading, so he departed in search of ale, bread and cheese while we remained, swaying, on the quayside, too weak to follow. When he finally returned, Bacon-face and I fairly tore into that bread, even though I knew my guts would revolt at the sudden abundance of food.

'Slowly, boys!' cautioned Da. Despite his warning, we ate like animals; ripping, tearing, arguing over the smallest morsel of cheese and gulping mouthfuls of cold ale until we finally slumped down on the harbour wall and vomited over the side into the Delaware River.

Da had also discovered there was to be an auction the following morning outside a coffee house on the east side of Front Street; household items, wagons and livestock, including horses, slaves and pigs.

'Slaves are sold as livestock?' I asked, wide-eyed. Da could only shrug his shoulders.

Weighed down by our sacks and blankets and me with the guns over my shoulders, we came upon Front Street with ease, thanks to Scuttle-Butt's directions, and settled down for the night on a planked walkway near the coffee house. Curling up under the tar cover, we watched the slow closing down of Philadelphia; keys jingling in locks as folk wished each other a pleasant evening and the last carts rumbling home. Drapes were drawn across windows and smoking chimneys threw cinders high into the black night. I pulled the cover tightly about my neck. I had never before slept on a street. Were thieves and robbers waiting in the shadows? If this had been Ireland, we would have lost everything including our undergarments.

Oil street lamps were lit, their golden haze reminding me of the night lamps on the ship, and I realised I missed the comforting creaking of the timbers and the rhythmic beat of the bow bouncing through the waves. I tried to sleep, but always some unfamiliar noise startled me; a dog barking, or the contents of a piss pot landing with a splash and a call to *shut the damn door!* In the soft light I could see Da was still awake and staring at the moon; the same moon that shone on Limavady and the dark, quiet fields of Ulster, and I was glad when sleep finally crept over me because I think he didn't want anyone to see the mist in his eyes.

Dawn brought noisy commotion; carts and carriages, and folk stepped out in elegant clothes. Ladies dressed their hair so finely I pitied Ma all the more, but she simply rammed her bonnet over her ears and called, 'Rouse yerselves! Come now, Lizzy, shake yerself girl!'

We groaned and stretched. Bacon-face was snoring like an old sow. 'Cease yer racket!' I hissed, landing the first thump of the day in his guts. His reply was a fast fist on my chin. We began most days like this.

'Bend yer ears to me now,' Da spoke in earnest, 'the auction will begin directly. It will be well attended so youse must close ranks and not lose yerselves.' I tried to heed his words, but unfortunately, I have always had an inclination to wander. Even when I was a bairn, Ma had to put a string around my waist and tie me to the door, afeared I would finish in Ballykelly.

I am unsure who took charge of the guns, or even at what moment my kin found themselves a good vantage point for the auction because a rich smell suddenly wafted past me from the coffee house and pulled me through the heavy, oak door. Inside, wisps of baccy smoke hung about the rafters and a host of gentlemen were engaged in lively discussion. Shrinking into the shadows behind the door, I hunkered down to observe this fascinating place. The talk was of trade winds and ships, of the price of coffee and a land of spices they called the Indies. A barmaid in cap and ruffled sleeves tipped black beans into a metal grinder and when she turned the handle, a crunching sound like hooves on gravel echoed noisily around the room. She then tipped the ground beans into a linen cloth, tied the top and lowered it into steaming water. Gradually that wonderful fragrance thickened until I was bathing in it.

I could have happily crouched behind the door for the rest of the day but for the young man who entered; a gentleman in a white necktie and brown jerkin, his well-cut dress with no patches or frayed cuffs. Searching the room for a vacant chair, his eyes fell on me.

'Well, upon my word, what have we here?' he exclaimed. His eyes roamed over my worn boots and ill-fitting garments. 'Do you have a name, boy?'

Struggling to my feet, I swept a hand through my hair, smoothed my shirt, and tried to speak as though I was someone of worth, 'William, sir. William Baxter.'

'William? As it happens, I have a son of that name, although he is a good deal younger than you. Do you reside here in Philadelphia, William Baxter?'

I shook my head. 'No, sir. I have lately arrived with my kin on the good ship *Mary* from Ireland.'

'Ireland, you say? And when did you last take nourishment?'

'Yesterday, sir.'

He didn't reply, instead, he reached into his top pocket and produced a shiny, silver coin and offered it to me. I was suddenly wary of the fellow. What did he want with me?

'Begging yer pardon, sir, but what service can I do in return? Deliver a message perhaps? Or have you need of yer horse, sir?'

His mouth twitched, a smile lurking at the corner of his lips. 'I require nothing, young man. I ask only that you purchase something to eat! Accept it in good faith,' he urged, 'I assure you there is nothing to fear.'

My grubby fingers quickly plucked the coin from his hand. 'Why, thank you kindly, sir!' This was a rare gift!

'Come, Mister Franklin!' beckoned a tall gentleman.

'Benjamin, sit with us!' cried another, and that good man disappeared amongst the puffed and powdered wigs. Grasping the coin, I breathed in the fragrance of that coffee house one last time, then scampered outside to find my kin.

'Ma! *Ma!*' Pushing my way through the crowds I found her watching the bidding with Thomas in her arms. Holding the coin high, I grinned proudly. 'Feast yer eyes on that, Ma!'

'William! Where have you been? This won't do! I was afeared we'd never again set eyes upon you!' Worry creased her forehead and I was sorry for it.

'I was in the coffee house,' I explained, 'and a gentleman gave me this coin asking no service in return!'

'Heavens above!' She shook her head in despair. 'We are but one day in this country and already you're a thief!'

'I didn't steal it!' I protested, 'it was given to me freely! The man desired nothing but that we buy some food!' Then I raced along the boardwalk to the bakery to follow his wishes.

Now, my da was a sharp bidder. He knew all about auctions as he'd been to many a sale in Londonderry. The language of an auction is a nod or a wink and he was accomplished in both. When the bidding was at an end he spat on his palm, shook the hand of the auctioneer and we made haste to claim our horse and cart. Only five horses remained, quietly biding their time. Some were too old to be wanted by anyone, while others were too young for a good day's work. One was a ten-year-old chestnut gelding.

'He stands fifteen hands and is well muscled – a good size for pulling a cart!' beamed Da.

'Has he a name?' asked Bacon-face.

'His name is Samson. What say you, boys! Is he not the most handsome horse you ever saw?'

Brushing my hand along the horse's flank, I breathed in his comforting sweet-grass scent. Steady eyes looked back at me from under thick, black lashes. We had owned only an old cob in Ireland, and although this lad was no fine carriage horse, I thought him a beauty. I met the stare in his dark eyes and somehow knew Samson would always be *my* horse. It was no matter who had paid for him; I would be his master. Those faithful eyes belonged to me.

Bacon-face helped me load the farm cart. It was not the sturdiest thing on two wheels – the iron rims had a right squeak on them – but as long as the planks held, Da was content. Ma perched Thomas and Lizzy on top of the seed bags, while Bacon-face and I marched alongside through a mire of mud called High Street, my guts fluttering with fear. Beyond the town lay nothing but forest and wild animals. We had only two fowling guns and Ma was useless with a weapon. She would more likely shoot us than any predator. That left Da and me to fend off any danger, which was a mite worrying as I reckoned most wild animals would be a good bit larger than me.

Thomas began to whine. Lizzy could do nothing with him – he needed sleep. Lifting his little, angry, squirming body, I tucked him against my shoulder where he gummed his thumb and snuggled, warm and blotchy against my neck. He at least was at peace. As for me, I was certain of only one thing; we were a long, long way from the shores of Ireland.

THE ATTACK

Lashing rain drenched us for the next three weeks. I truly believe it followed us from Ireland out of sheer spite, angry at us for daring to leave the shores of Ulster. It smacked the tarred cover while the young'uns huddled underneath, water dribbling down their necks. We hacked down branches, heaved the cart over tree stumps, around rocks and through swollen streams, levering branches under the wheels to free them from the bubbling mud, while a tide of brown sludge seeped into our boots and dripped from the hem of Ma's dress. Lizzy fell face down in the mire and had to be dipped in a river, and Thomas had to be carried, or stay in the cart, so he wasn't best pleased, especially as he was learning to walk.

We also discovered Samson didn't like thunder. That horse was good-natured until the sky rumbled, then he became the devil's steed. Bucking and rearing, he crashed through the trees, dragging the cart behind him while we gave chase; Lizzy gripping Thomas and screaming in terror. We lost a wheel, but thankfully there were no injuries. After that, there was only one solution; to cover Samson's eyes with a neckerchief when it thundered so he couldn't see where he was going.

On the first sunny morning since leaving Philadelphia, Da stopped by the edge of a creek, put his hands on his hips, and surveyed a wide, flat valley stretching lush and green into the distance. Walking a little way through the trees, he stamped the ground with his big, black boots to gauge the firmness of the soil, then broke the earth with the shovel and let the dark, damp dirt crumble through his fingers. The smell of warm grass took me back to haymaking time in the fields of Limavady, and the fresh scent of pine trees steaming in the warm sun reminded me of spruce trees along the Roe valley. This would be a grand place to settle; it smelled of home. If any man gained profit from this valley, we gave no thought to it because no dwelling had been built and the soil had not been worked. This was our promised land; there for the taking. So we took it.

By the beginning of winter, we had cleared enough scrub and trees to build a small, windowless, birch-lapped crib house with a lean-to stable for Samson. Da had plans to build a larger cabin in the spring with a proper hearth and a porch to sit under in the evenings. Before the ground became hard with frost, Bacon-face and I split lengths of wood with a beetle and wedge and helped Da fence our first field. With Samson's help, we ploughed and seeded the rich soil knowing there was little time to waste, and we were proved right. Only two weeks later, winter pounced, howling like a white wolf, biting into our bundled-up bodies and gripping the creek until the water froze beneath its claws. It snapped branches with bone-breaking ferocity, dripped icicles along the crib house roof and left deep, dangerous drifts in its wake. I had never seen snow like that in Ireland, but we didn't shrink from its fangs. We hunted with traps, smashed holes in the icy river and caught bass and perch, only using the fowling guns if we had a clear shot as, once fired, every animal for miles fled; there was no second chance. We even ate beaver. The meat tasted like tough, greasy beef but was very welcome at our table, especially the tail, which Thomas sucked on for days to soothe his gums.

On bitter winter evenings, Da would sit with a nip of something that, if taken in large amounts, could make a man blind. So he said. Ma always sat too close to the fire; her woollen stockings rolled around her ankles and her mottled veins like the rivers of Ulster. But our harsh life in Ireland had prepared us well for Penn's country. We could have survived on our own spit.

As the days lengthened, a warm southern breeze chased away the snow. Bluebells and little purple irises peeped from the shade of the evergreen trees, and single, green, oat shoots broke through the soil and stretched for the sun. Almost without realising it, we had settled into our new life. I explored every turn in the creek for miles until the hills and valleys became familiar. Sometimes Bacon-face and I went deer hunting with Da, and other times I just crouched downwind from the big, snorting bucks as they paced around their territory, sniffing the air and rounding up their young does. As spring turned to summer, most of my days were spent chopping wood, helping Da finish the new cabin, and watering the crops and vegetables in the cool of the evening.

Ma was delighted with our new home. At one end of the cabin, a stone chimney climbed to the roof, the clay hearth like a wide, grey puddle on the dirt floor. At the other end lay hemp sacks filled with dry grass, where we slept like animals packed in a burrow. While I helped Da make a small table, four three-legged stools and two chairs, Ma made squat bush fruit candles and dried all manner of berries on the roof in the sun, then strung them inside along the beams. The whole place looked right homely.

Eventually, the oats we had planted grew tall and swayed golden, telling us it was harvest time. Da and I scythed row after row until my spine felt twisted out of shape and weeping blisters covered my right hand. Even tying my neckerchief around the wounds couldn't dull the pain, and I sank to the ground with relief when Bacon-face and Lizzy finally gathered the last oat-sheaf, and our work was finished. Pleased with our efforts and the good harvest, we lay straight-backed at last in the shade of the cabin and drank warm ale. If our peaceful life had only remained in that happy state, we would have been content, but autumn came early that year and with it, disaster.

One afternoon, when the swallows had flown away and the ploughed fields rolled like brown, feathered quilts, I spied a wolf skinnier than a rat's tail crouched beneath a hickory tree not thirty yards from the cabin; its tawny coat flashing among the red and gold leaves. Slowly, I hunkered down until I was level with its wide, grey eyes. This was no full-grown wolf. It was a young'un, sleek and hungry. Now, I'd wanted a dog since I was a bairn, but wondered if a wolf might prove just as loyal.

Ma came to the door of the cabin, her workaday black dress speckled with flour where she'd forgotten her apron. Leaning against the cabin wall, she wiped her chicken-wringing hands on an old cloth.

'There's a wolf in the trees,' I whispered, 'it looks fair starved.'

She reached for the fowling guns that always sat under the porch, but I held up a hand. 'Wait, Ma. It's a young wolf. I got a mind to try and tame it. I know we have little food to spare, but I reckon I'll set out a bone – see if it will come close.'

Ducking inside the cabin, I snatched a gnawed-down-to-nothing rabbit bone from the table, ran to the fence, and placed it on a shard of bluestone. The wolf watched, sniffing the breeze, catching the scent. It wouldn't leave the trees while I was nearby, so I ran back to the fields; there was always plenty of work to occupy my time. The last of the ripe, orange pumpkins still lay in the fields among a tangle of yellowing leaves, so I set about storing them in the crib house, then took up the long-handled axe; chopping firewood was a never-ending task. We needed dry wood for the coming winter, but also wood seasoned for at least a twelvemonth for the following winters. Ma came outside and leant against a porch post in the afternoon sun, her arms folded and ankles crossed, sometimes she would snatch a few moments to herself while Thomas was asleep. Shading her eyes, she scanned the trees. 'That bone has gone, William!'

With a hefty thud, I drove the axe into the top of a tree stump and ran to the porch where I could see for myself. At that moment, Bacon-face came skipping past the water barrel, licking his fingers, and took the two steps up onto the porch in one leap. I glared at him. 'What are you sucking? Open yer gob!'

'Na!'

I leapt on him, punching and kicking. 'A thief is what you are, James Baxter!'

'No one calls me a thief!'

'Yer a fibbing wee brat!'

'I got a right to take food if I see it! There was still gristle on that bone!'

We tumbled from the porch onto the dry, dusty dirt, scattering the chickens in a whirl of feathers. I thumped him in the guts – hard. He barely winced. Grabbing a handful of dirt, he flung it in my face. I spat back brown saliva, mashing it between his lips. We screeched and squirmed until two hands, well used to our brawling, pulled us apart by the lugs.

'Boys! My patience is pared to the bone!' cried Ma. 'You bait each other like two young cockerels! William, away with you and set the rabbit snares! James – yer da needs help with a cartwheel! This is yer final warning, lads! Keep yerselves apart or youse will get a good belting!'

Grabbing my jacket from inside the cabin, I rammed my arms into the sleeves, shoved my gloves in the pockets and spat a final curse at Bacon-face, 'You thieving toad!' There were times he made me wild. Snatching the snares from the post-peg, I grabbed one of the fowling guns, the powder horn and shot pouch, and marched off to saddle Samson.

Still fuming and muttering oaths, I rode up through the tall pine trees until I was high above the settlement where the cool, clean smell of wild mint mingled with oak smoke rising from the chimney. I knew every inch of these woods and every animal prowling within them. I knew how to smoke out the honeybees and steal a finger of sticky honeycomb from their hive. I knew where to find the juiciest blackberries, which hollow tree held a pine marten nest, and where the old, grey fox had its den.

Tethering Samson, I skirted the trees and by the time I'd set the snares, the light was already fading. It would soon be time for the evening meal and I knew I mustn't linger, but after the fight with Bacon-face, I was enjoying the peace. Placing the fowler, horn and shot pouch at the foot of a large maple tree, I stretched out and gazed up through crimson autumn leaves at the darkening sky.

A vague feeling of alarm tingled the back of my neck. I sat up, listening, an uneasy feeling knotting my guts. Around me, the forest had suddenly stopped breathing. The screeching gulls come lately for the winter had quieted. The jeer of the blue jays was silent. Even the little robins had hushed their chirring. The steady chatter and hum of the woods had simply disappeared. Scrambling to a nearby ridge, I peered down at the settlement below on the flat land. The candles weren't yet lit as the day's work was still unfinished. Ma was sitting under the porch gutting fish, a board on her lap and her dress hanging like a sail between her knees. Thomas, awake after his nap, was playing in the dirt, while Lizzy happily pounded her Sunday apron in the wide washing barrel. Bacon-face was dragging one of the heavy cartwheels to the river to swell the shrunken wood so it would fit the iron rim, while

Da painted hot tar on the planked under-seams to help make the cart watertight for the winter.

A sudden squawking tightened every muscle in my body. A blizzard of black, beating feathers burst from the trees near the river. My throat closed tight as a barnacle. Something had startled the crows. It couldn't be a bear. Bears don't creep. They blunder. It couldn't be a mountain lion either because they hunt at night. That left only one possibility, a thought so dreadful, clammy sweat bathed me like morning dew. I had to warn Da, but I could barely breathe let alone shout, and even if I tried, I feared my voice wouldn't carry the distance. There was only one thing to do; fire a warning shot.

Scrambling back to the maple tree, I grabbed the fowler and with trembling fingers, tipped black powder from the horn down the barrel. The wad. Where was the wad? I couldn't ram down the shot without it. I rummaged in my pockets but found only my gloves. *I'd forgotten the wad.* Ragged breath. Clawing panic!

Ma's sudden shriek chilled my blood. The fowler fell from my hands. Stumbling back to the ridge, I stared down again at the settlement. Six Natives, half-naked, painted and armed with bows and axes, were splashing through the creek toward the cabin. Da threw down the pot of tar. Dashing toward the porch, he shouted a warning. Fish guts scattered as Ma grabbed Thomas and stumbled into the cabin. James and Lizzy tumbled in behind her. Da snatched the remaining fowler from the porch, threw himself across the threshold, and slammed the door.

The Natives leapt up the porch steps. Finding the door bolted, they hammered on the wood. Inside the cabin, someone fired the fowler. The shot went straight through the door leaving a jagged, blackened hole smouldering in the planks. A Native staggered, then toppled from the porch onto the dirt, a pool of crimson blood widening across his dark flesh. His brothers stared in disbelief.

They tried to rouse him; to save him. Turning furiously toward the cabin, they kicked in the door. A storm of splintered wood flew across the porch. The piercing screams of my kin shredded the air as everything we owned – furniture, pots and bowls – crashed against the walls. It was the sound of my life being smashed to pieces.

My heart punched like a beast trying to escape. My lungs begged for air. Sparks whirled inside my head. I crumpled to my knees as fiery food rushed up my gullet, then retched until my sides ached, lurching like a pecking chicken, stifling sobs for fear of discovery, terrified they might find me. When the vomiting finally stopped, I began to rock back and forth; dumb, senseless, rocking, like a demented mother with a dead child. Like Ma when she lost my baby sisters. I didn't stop until a blister of blood dripped on my jacket, and I realised I had bitten right through my bottom lip.

The settlement was now eerily quiet. All I could think about was getting back down to the cabin to see if anyone had survived. Natives are not known for their mercy, yet I clung to the hope my kin had somehow escaped death. The hour was already late, even now darkness walled the eastern sky, yet the urge to reach my family was so overwhelming that I began stumbling down through the shadowy trees. Almost immediately I lost the path, but couldn't stop; I *had* to reach the cabin. With barely enough light to see my own hands, common sense told me this was folly; I would do myself an injury, but I paid no heed. Tripping over dead branches and tangled undergrowth, I staggered on in the deepening twilight until suddenly I missed my footing and hurtled, screaming with fright, down through the trees. Scratched and bleeding, I finally slid to a halt in a gulley, where I lay breathless in the dirt, wretched with fury at my failure. How far I'd fallen I couldn't say, but the final, faint tapers of daylight soon disappeared, leaving the woods as black as a bog – darkness so thick I could have sliced it with a knife.

Sanity is a slippery devil, and I must have been half-mad with grief to think I could find my way down the hillside in the dark. Lying there in that pitiful state something unexpected slithered into my thoughts and clung to me like a leech; *guilt*. Their deaths were *my* fault. Why had I not heeded Da? How many times had he told me to load the fowler *before* going into the woods? If I'd fired the weapon, they may have had time to escape, but the fight with James had riled me so much I'd forgotten all the rules. I tried to rise above the guilt, but it burrowed under my skin like a tick, then seeped into my bones like a disease and made itself at home.

A sudden, low, whinny broke the silence. Samson!

'Where are you, boy? Here! Come, boy!'

I listened for the thump of his hooves and his snuffles and snorts as he strained against his tethered rein to free himself. Then following the sounds, I clawed my way out of the gulley and back up the hillside, feeling my way around the trees like a blind man, until finding Samson at last, I flung my arms around his warm, strong neck. His soft, velvet muzzle nibbled my hair and I was grateful for his steady presence in my lonely world.

'Samson, there is only you and me now, boy,' I sobbed. 'There are no candles burning in the cabin. No light through the cracks in the door or cinders floating from the chimney. Not even the glow of Da's pipe under the porch. If they *are* dead, where am I to go? What am I to do?'

I wished I had a dog; a hound so faithful it would wag its tail right off at the sight of me. I wouldn't be so afeared with such an animal by my side, but it was too late to moan about that now. The hot vomit had ripped a layer of skin from my throat. I was plagued with thirst, but if I couldn't reach the cabin in the dark, I certainly stood little chance of finding the river. In any case, the Dullahans would now be out hunting; those headless fiends who ride black, fire-breathing horses and take the souls of poor folk waiting for death. Grandma had warned me about them. Well, they wouldn't get a hold of me, at least not tonight.

Hauling the saddle and horse blanket to the ground, I wrapped myself in the hairy, woollen cover, breathing in the familiar smell of saddle leather, and lay down on a bed of dry leaves. Even though Samson was tethered near me, he was invisible in the vast darkness, the jangle from his bridle my only comfort and reassurance that he was close by. And that was the last sound I heard before exhaustion dragged me into night terrors where Da was bellowing a storm at me for not loading the fowler.

ALONE

In that strange, ethereal place between sleeping and waking, I thought I heard Ma slosh steaming clabber into a trencher and call me to eat, but as daylight flickered beneath my lashes, memories of the attack returned like foul-tasting medicine that I could neither spit out nor swallow.

Thin, spidery shafts of sunlight flooded through the trees. It was only a little after dawn, but my desperation to get to the cabin was still as fierce and I couldn't wait a moment longer. Perhaps I had accidentally eaten thorn apple and it had given me a ghastly hallucination. I would find Ma bristling like a cat, hand raised to give me a good slap for sleeping in the woods and worrying her half to death.

Quickly, I spread the blanket over Samson's back, settled the saddle on top and tightened the girth. My mouth was dry as sand; every swallow like shards of glass in my throat, but finding water would have to wait. Slinging the fowler across my back, I hung the powder horn and shot pouch from the saddle cantle, looped the reins through my fingers and hurriedly made my way back down through the trees.

The woods that had barred me last night were now full of bird song, but I didn't stop to listen. With Samson's heavy hooves thudding behind me, I tugged him along the path toward the crib house and tethered his reins to a fence post, my chest heaving with relief that so far, I was safe. Crouching down, I surveyed the area for signs of danger, straining for the sound of voices – any voices. The settlement had been my home for over a year, often rowdy, sometimes calm, but never like this – as silent as a tomb. The busy sounds of everyday life I was used to were missing; Ma shaking out the bed sacking and stamping on the bark beetles, Lizzy sweeping the floor, James gathering wood for the fire and Thomas, sweet little Thomas, running around with his soggy, night rag hanging between his knees.

Sprinting across the grass to the side of the cabin, I peered around the corner. Lizzy's apron was floating in the washing barrel. The pot of tar, spilt where Da had dropped it, leaked a narrow, shiny, black stream through the grass.

'Ma? Da? Is anyone there?' My voice seemed to come from the bottom of a barrel; hollow, echoing in the stillness. There was no reply. With my back to the wall, I stepped up onto the porch. Around my feet, splinters of door frame lay like kindling and the air reeked of rotting fish; Ma had been cleaning perch when the Natives came, and the guts were now a buzzing mass of black flies. Hesitantly, I tiptoed along the porch. Where the Native died, a dark stain of dry blood puddled the planks. I had no desire to step in it. Hugging the wall, I inched my way toward the door. It hung open on one hinge, the smashed latch still attached to the wood. My heart bounced loose in my chest. Spit dried on my tongue. Trembling, I peeped around the shattered door frame into the gloom.

A shroud of silence held me motionless. I could see only shapes at first; scattered fragments; broken chairs, table legs and smashed bowls. Dark splatters whipped the walls. A heap of clothes lay tucked in a tight mound as though someone was sleeping. As my eyes grew accustomed, that heap became the bloody body of my da; a deep slash across the back of his neck that must have severed it to the bone. I let slip a sob. Or perhaps it was a scream. I could no longer tell. Beside him lay James. There was barely a scratch on my brother. Only the speckled smudge of blood on the left side of his shirt showed where a knife had entered his body. To the right of the hearth lay Lizzy, pale as moonlight, the top of her head smothered in dark, mashed blackberries. For a moment I couldn't understand what had happened to her, then I realised she'd been scalped.

My legs jellied. A tide of wretchedness threw me backward from the doorway! I crashed into one of the porch posts, but the ordeal was not yet finished. Where was Ma? Where was Thomas? My horrified gaze fell on a piece of Ma's black shawl snagged on the bottom of the door. A small, chubby, grey hand poked from beneath it; Thomas! Ma must have hidden with him behind the door! She must be lying there still! My eyes swept wildly, hysterically around the room. There was nowhere else she could be! A sudden chilling thought swept through me – if they had scalped Lizzy, what had they done to Ma? I couldn't bear to see her poor maimed and disfigured body. I wasn't brave enough. I wasn't James – he would have looked, but I didn't have even a whisper of my brother's courage. I wanted to scream until I had no more breath. To close my eyes and never again open them.

Stumbling from the porch, I fled back toward the crib house. I had to get away from this place; from this hell! My foot caught on something in the grass. Landing with a thump, I saw it was Da's Sunday belt. What was it doing here? Then I remembered Thomas had found it in the cabin yesterday, and dragged it around like a toy. What a telling-off he would have had if Da had caught him. Clutching the soft leather, I breathed in the familiar smell as memories surged; deer hunting with Da, fishing together, smoking his pipe until I almost coughed up my guts. In a fit of despair, I raised the belt high above my head, then walloped the earth with such force it drew a howl from my throat. I whipped that ground, lashing into it over and over until the buckle tore up the soil and blades of shredded grass flew around me. I thrashed until sweat slid down my back. I pounded out my misery until the muscles in my arms begged me to stop, then I collapsed, wet-cheeked and weary on the puckered earth. My whole body ached for my grandma, the pain sharper than any jagged wound. I longed to throw my arms around her and hide against her heartbeat.

The smell of yellow meadowsweet, marsh marigold and golden gorse suddenly drifted by me. I knew their fragrance well, they were the flowers Grandma used to dye yarn, but they weren't in bloom in autumn and even if they had been, there were none near me.

The fragrance was faint at first, as though a wealthy, perfumed lady had passed nearby, but soon it grew as strong as a field of flowers. It swept up my nose and burst, upon my senses. It wrapped around me like an invisible hug, clinging to my skin. I could even smell it on my hair and taste it on my tongue. Filling my lungs, I tried to hold onto it, but I may as well have tried to grasp a rainbow or the sun as it dances on the waves. The more I frantically inhaled, the more the fragrance faded, until it disappeared completely and I was once again alone on the grass.

Now, I have no understanding of how witches work, but somehow, I knew Grandma had heard my cries. Her spirit had dipped me in a scent I would recognise and called me home. How such a thing could happen, I couldn't say, but then Grandma had many strange gifts. She told me that when she was a girl, she'd been attacked by gypsies who tried to pull out her teeth – real teeth are valuable. Yet, almost as soon as those wild women had grabbed her hair and produced their pliers, they let her go, startled, as though they recognised in Grandma something much more powerful than their own miserable talent for reading palms. If she had the power to talk to the dead, who weren't even of this world, then perhaps she also had the power to send her spirit across an ocean. All I know is that her perfume gave me the courage I so badly needed to struggle again to my feet. I knew now where I should go, home to Ireland. It would take all of my determination because the journey would mean weeks of riding through dangerous forests all the way back to the port at Philadelphia, but it seemed a good plan, a sensible plan. I would need to prepare for such a journey though, and do it quickly. My chances of survival would be slim unless I had some way of catching food. Da had stored certain items high on the beams in the crib house in case of any *unforeseen situation*. I was fairly certain this was one of those situations.

Snatching the belt, I raced back across the grass only to find the crib house, which we had used for storage, almost empty. Our harvested food – oats, pumpkins and beans – had been taken by the Natives. Scrape marks clawed the dirt where the barrel of molasses and the cask of gunpowder had been dragged outside. Even the scythes had been taken from the wall pegs. All that remained was a wooden ladder with two broken rungs, one ripped sack that oozed oats like a weeping wound and the old pan Ma used for collecting eggs; one smashed egg lying on the ground like a yellow, crinkled sun in a sky of dry slime.

Scooping up an armful of oats from the ripped sack, I tossed them outside for Samson, leaving him to grind the grain between his large molars. Next, I quickly buckled Da's belt around my jacket, then, setting the ladder against a high cross-beam, climbed above the broken rungs until I could reach the dry, dusty timbers. Running my fingers along the wood, I found a small axe, spare flints, a knife, gun wads and fish hooks. Thrusting the axe and knife under my belt, I shoved the other items into my pockets and jumped back down to the ground. On a wall peg behind the door hung two large, rabbit-skin bags and strings of rabbit sinew, all unseen by the Natives. I hurriedly filled one bag with oats. The second bag still held our family Bible and Sunday leather water bottle, so I stuffed the old pan and strings of sinew in on top and hung both bags over the saddle cantle, driven only by a frantic desire to escape the settlement.

Taking one last look at the cabin, I realised someone should be told about what had happened here, but who? We had no neighbours. The nearest settlement was a two-hour ride. The only person I could think of was Reverend Bertram, the minister at Derry Session House; a log cabin used as a church and named after Londonderry. It lay about an hour's journey from the settlement. Reverend Bertram may even bury my kin, a thought which gave me some relief, as otherwise they would be eaten by wild animals.

It was time to go. Tugging Samson back along the path toward the forest, a fragment of white linen suddenly whirled past me on the breeze and caught on a branch, flapping like a small flag of surrender. It was the piece of old, frayed bodice Ma had used to protect her little silver jug. The Natives must have found her treasure. Snatching the cloth, I smoothed the fibres with my fingers and breathed in the dank, musty odour of fabric kept at the bottom of a wooden box. It was instantly precious to me, something that belonged to Ma, but there was no time to dwell on the find because the rising wind was whipping blood-red leaves around my ankles. Slipping the little piece of cloth safely into the pocket of my breeches, I climbed up on the saddle. Winter was approaching like a wolf on a scent and already nipping at my heels. I knew I must make haste. I couldn't waste a single day because cold is as dangerous an enemy as any Native, and the bitter snows would soon be upon me.

DERRY CHURCH

I knew the path well to Derry Session House because every second Sunday, Da would hook up the cart and we'd trundle along the rutted road to praise the Lord. While he said it was good for the soul to attend worship, we also looked forward to sharing news with other folks. Life on the settlement could be lonely, and when the whole company assembled, there was all manner of blether, particularly from the women. Ma hardly drew breath from the moment we arrived.

The track flowed like a crumpled dried-up riverbed; waves of thick, brown wheel-furrows banking the sides. I saddle-swayed along the ruts with the smell of damp bark and pea-green moss seeping up my nostrils. I had a thirst that raged like a beast. Samson must also have been desperate for water. I knew at some point I would cross a stream, but mile after dry-mouthed mile passed with no sign of it until, at last, I spied a gentle, sparkling thread of silver.

Sliding quickly from the saddle, I threw myself down at the water's edge, plunged my face into the cold stream, and greedily gulped mouthfuls that eased my thirst and soothed my throat, then lay on the bank spluttering and coughing, as Samson slurped beside me. It seemed a peaceful place. Black-capped chickadees were singing in the trees and a little way along the bank, two blue herons spread their long toes and walked in slow, careful strides. Nearby, fat, ripe cranberries hung on woody stems. I loved their sharp, juicy taste, but even though they were a favourite, I couldn't have forced a single berry down my throat. Hurriedly, I filled the water bottle, knowing I shouldn't remain long in these woods. Natives could be hiding in the trees like a pack of wolves, watching my every move. If I hadn't been so thirsty, I would never have stopped here, miles from anywhere. In the short time since the attack, I had already learned to be increasingly wary and not make myself a target. Some ancient instinct was teaching me how to keep myself safe – and it was not safe to stay here. It was time to leave this lonely spot.

Derry Session House finally came into view, and I was glad to see its familiar, thick, un-lapped boards. Reverend Bertram also held reading lessons. I'd been to the classes myself to learn reading and writing. I hoped he would be at home, so I was relieved to see him chopping wood and reminded myself to be polite and well mannered as my parents would have wished, Reverend Bertram was a man of letters and had silver buckles on his shoes.

At the sound of hooves, he raised his head, squinted against the morning sun and called, 'Ah, William Baxter! Good day to you, young sir! What brings you this way?'

As I drew near, he could see my red eyes and tear-stained cheeks. Throwing down the axe he hurried toward me, his brow knotted with concern. 'Whatever ails you, boy?'

Dismounting, I gave a respectful nod. 'Good day, Reverend Bertram. I come with fearful bad tidings. Natives attacked the settlement yesterday. They killed my kin; Ma and Da and my brothers and sister.'

His face turned grey as old pan grease. He struggled for words, which seemed odd to me considering the length of his sermons.

'It caused me such a terrible fright I'm not done shaking, sir,' I stammered.

Guiding me by the shoulder, he beckoned me toward the house. 'Come inside. Come, William. Tell me all that has happened.'

Following him through the low, wooden door into the warmth, I sat on a chair by the ink-blotched table. The room was as I remembered; mud-chinked walls stained with wood smoke. That day he was burning cherry wood for I know the sweet fragrance of that lovely tree. I used to sit here for my reading lessons beside a boy called Richard Campbell, who often nudged my arm so I would lose my place on the page. The reverend near cut that boy's knuckles off with a cane. Richard Campbell didn't come again after that.

Reverend Bertram brought ale and a small plate of cold, sliced duck, placed it before me, then sat opposite, hands clasped.

'Forgive me, sir, but I got no appetite.' I pushed the plate toward the middle of the table. 'I'm only alive because I was in the woods, so escaped with my life.'

He listened intently, the skin around his lips drawn into small, thin lines, then asked quietly, 'Do you know which tribe were responsible for this outrage?'

'They were painted and carried weapons, but I can't recall their faces or anything of their garments.'

'It's the shock, William. The mind shields us from things too dreadful to dwell upon for the present.'

'Will it always be so?'

He hesitated. 'Perhaps. You must give yourself time. Such memories can't be forced.'

'But to murder an entire family – have you ever heard of such a thing?'

'No, in truth I have not, although we walk a delicate line. There is much tension. Natives have been known to kill the livestock of settlers without touching a single morsel for food. There have been so many rumours about attacks that some settlers have abandoned their lands in fear.' His brow furrowed and he steepled his fingers as if in prayer. 'William, may I ask something that requires a reply of the utmost honesty?'

'I will answer any question as truthfully as I am able, sir.'

'Were the Natives brandishing their weapons when they crossed the creek?'

I tried to remember, replying hastily, 'They were carrying weapons so they surely meant to kill us!'

'It's usual for them to carry weapons, William. They always carry bows, arrows and often an axe. Were they shouting threats?'

'No, but – they came right up to the cabin!'

'And when they came to the porch, they knocked on the door?'

'They hammered on it!' I was sweating, unsure if it was the recalling of such horror, or if I needed to take off my jacket because of the warm fire. 'Then someone – Da most likely – fired a shot through the door and killed one of the Natives.'

Startled, Reverend Bertram's outsized eyes stared back at me. 'Your father *killed* a Native?'

My lashes clumped with moisture. 'The Native – he fell from the porch with his chest covered in blood! Then the others kicked in the door!'

A small gasp escaped his lips. For a moment we sat in silence; me in fury and him grappling with the seriousness of my words. At length, he asked, 'Were the Natives surprised by the shot?'

'Indeed they were, sir!'

He covered his eyes with his hands, and when he spoke his voice was low and trembling, 'I fear there has been a terrible misunderstanding, William.'

'Misunderstanding?' I cried. 'No! I saw it happen!'

'William, listen to me. Several years ago two white men – Walter and John Winter – killed three Natives.'

He had my attention.

'There was some confusion as the men believed a family of settlers were under attack. They had heard rumours of such attacks over by Tulpehocken, so were barricading their homes when the son of a neighbour arrived saying Natives had come to his father's house. Now, bearing in mind Walter and John Winter believed the rumours from Tulpehocken, they grabbed their muskets, followed the boy to his home and killed the three Natives; one man and two women. However, it soon became clear these Natives were not attacking the home, but simply wanted information. Walter and John Winter were hanged for the crime.' He sighed. 'I'm telling you this to show the nervousness of settlers. The problem is that we are not accustomed to Native ways. This has been their land for many hundreds of years. They go where they wish without asking permission and can be very unnerving when they appear armed and painted.'

There was a lump as big as a boulder in my throat.

'I can't be certain,' he continued, 'but settlers are so nervous of all Natives that another misunderstanding was bound to occur. It is to be deeply regretted.'

'My da wouldn't kill someone by mistake!' I insisted.

'I believe he truly thought his life was in danger,' he hurriedly replied, 'and the Natives may also have been the worse for alcohol. White traders sell them rum and they lose their heads on it. Chiefs and tribal leaders have asked for no more trade in alcohol because their stupefied warriors fight and kill each other, and sell everything they own to feed their desire for more liquor.'

I knew his argument was well meant, but it wouldn't stand with me. Pushing back the chair I whirled toward the door.

'Wait!' He hurried after me. 'Forgive me, William, but what has happened will spread alarm through all the settlers in the area. Our relationship with the Natives is already strained. We must not anger them with falsehoods or accuse them with untruths. Come,' he helped me again to the table, 'we will speak of it no more.'

41

Confused and angry, I slumped back down onto the chair. I cared not a farthing if there had been a 'misunderstanding'. I hated Natives with a loathing that gnawed at my very soul and anything he said wasn't going to change that. I didn't argue further with him, not because it would be rude, but because I needed his help with another matter.

'May I beg you to do something for me, sir?' I ventured.

'You have but to ask, William.'

'The names of my kin are written in our Bible. I can read and write because you yerself taught me, but I don't have a fine writing hand. Pray, sir, will you add the year against their names? I fear I'm too clumsy. Someday I hope to return it to my kin in Ireland and I don't want it a muddle of ink and stain.'

'Of course, William, it's the least I can do. Go, fetch your Bible.'

Outside, I lifted the book from the bag, then again took my place at the table as he crossed to a small, rough cabinet. Inside were rolls of vellum, a few well-thumbed books, a piece of stained rag, various quills and a small, earthen pot of ink. Placing the necessary items on the table, he opened the Bible and began to read the first page:

'**Henry Baxter** born 1671. Married Leah Campbell 1694.
'Issue: **John Baxter** born 1698. Married Ruby Allen 1721.
'Issue: **William** 1722
'**James** 1724
'**Elizabeth** 1727
'**Anne** 1728. Died age 1 year and 3 months. Diphtheria.
'**Abigail** 1731. Died age 3 months. Failure to thrive.
'**Thomas** 1734.'

Dipping a quill in the ink, he dabbed the excess on the rag, then carefully began to write beside each name, 'Died 1736.' There was only one sound in that quiet place; the scratch of the quill, and to see the date there before me, made their deaths so final I had to wipe a sleeve across my eyes. The reverend blew gently on the paper to dry the ink, laid down the quill, and looked steadily at me. 'You are welcome to bide with us awhile. It isn't good to be alone with such grief.'

'I thank you, sir, but you got mouths enough to feed. In truth, I want to return to Ireland. I hope to reach Philadelphia then work for passage, so I must put a good many miles behind me by nightfall, although I am grateful for yer kind offer.'

'Philadelphia is a good undertaking, a hundred miles or thereabouts. That's a fair journey for a young lad.'

'Reckon so, but if I want to go home, I got no choice.' I fiddled nervously with the buckle on Da's belt. 'Sir, if I may be so bold, there is one more thing. My kin still lie in the cabin. I couldn't bury them on my own, I don't have the strength to even lift my da.'

'Have no fear, William, I will gather some men this very afternoon and we will go to the settlement and do what is necessary.'

I sank back in the chair with relief. 'I'm much obliged. I can't bear the thought of them being eaten by animals.'

'You needn't be concerned about such a thing. I knew your parents well and will give them a proper and dignified burial. Is there anywhere in particular you would like them laid?'

Only one place came to mind. We were hardy people, and if there was even a hint of sunshine, we ate outside rather than in the gloom of the cabin. 'There is a large oak tree at the corner of the bean field. I think they would like it there.'

Tucking the Bible under my arm, we walked back outside into the sunshine. He held out his hand to me and declared, 'You are the man now, William.' But shaking his hand didn't make me feel more of a man. It only made me feel all the more lonely. 'You are welcome to return should the need arise. God works in strange ways, m'boy. Try to remember that.'

'Thank you kindly, sir, but I don't think I like His ways.' I suppose it was rude of me, but I was exhausted and frayed at the edges. With those final words, I shoved the Bible back in the bag, settled in the saddle, and turned Samson toward the Susquehanna River, leaving the lone figure of Reverend Bertram waving among fluttering autumn leaves in the morning sun.

ERIK

Ma used to say, 'if you can't pluck feathers, don't kill a chicken'.

She would spout many a strange saying, but unfortunately, never explained their meaning. My best guess was, 'don't attempt something if you have no skill for the work'. Apart from trapping rabbits and catching the occasional fish, I had little by way of survival skills, yet here I was, attempting something that would make a grown man hesitate. What would Ma think of my plan? If only I could ask her.

Riding through that dense forest, I thought of Ma's words until they so occupied my thoughts, I was able to rise above my constant fear that Natives may be watching me, ready to pounce at any moment. When I came again to the creek where the cranberries grew, I followed it south, stopping by the water's edge when the sun was overhead to gather a few fallen nuts; cracking the shells with the handle of my knife. But I didn't linger, there are many dangers in the forest for a boy alone.

Now, it may have been the warmth of the sun or my weariness, but gradually my eyes felt as though lead weights were hanging from my lashes. My head drooped, and somewhere along that trail, I drifted into sleep. What kind of idiotic person falls asleep on a horse! I might have been attacked by wild animals, or even Natives! How long I slept, I couldn't say, but suddenly I awoke, cold, hungry, and startled to find the sun had slipped low in the sky and I was without a safe resting place for the night.

Tall, shadowy pines stared silently down at me. What place was this? Where was the river path? Swivelling in the saddle I searched for the track, but every direction looked the same. Samson must have wandered at will through the trees for hours. I was completely lost! I'd been in the saddle only one day and already botched it! The dark was rising. What should I do? Which way should I go? *Which way!*

A hint of wood smoke suddenly tickled my nose. The smell was unmistakable, but was it from a cabin – or a Native campfire? Slipping quietly from the saddle, I tethered Samson to a branch and inched my way through the trees. The sound of crackling wood grew sharper with every step until I could see the flickering flames of a campfire. Trembling, I crouched behind a large pine tree and peered through its prickly branches.

In a small clearing, a man dressed in furs was sitting on a log, skinning a rabbit. Blond hair, straight as straw, poked from the flaps of his beaver hat, giving him the appearance of a scarecrow. He had the biggest nose I had ever seen, a cliff shading a sea of stubble. In truth, his entire face looked as though it had been carelessly thrown together by an apprentice potter. I took him to be about the age of Da, but that was the only similarity because this man was huge. Even seated his knees almost touched his chin.

A stallion, black as a pot boiled dry, stood untethered near his master, the reins swept over the saddle. A second, smaller horse carried a heap of pelts, while around the man's large feet lay all manner of wares; a leather water bottle, glass beads, copper kettles, fish hooks, knives, a bundle of linen shirts and a roll of sky-blue cloth. The black horse suddenly snorted. Lifting its head, it stamped a large front hoof on the dry earth then turned its thick neck in my direction. I knew the jig was up because the signal was instantly understood by its master. Carefully, he laid down the rabbit, reached for his musket and rose to his feet. He was a fortress on legs. I would have to be guarded. There wasn't a soul to protect me now. I had to protect myself.

'Who is there?' His voice boomed like a blast of buckshot. I tried to rise slowly from my hiding place, but the writhing ants in my guts got the better of me and I thrust my hands in the air and stood to attention as though someone had put a rod down my spine.

'I beg you, sir – don't shoot! I'm unarmed!'

He hesitated, his eyes roaming the trees for more intruders. 'Are you alone?'

'I am, sir! My kin were killed by Natives. I'm trying to reach Philadelphia, but I got no place to sleep. I would be grateful if I could share yer fire.'

His bird-egg-blue eyes narrowed like a squashed summer sky. 'Your folk have been killed you say?'

I faltered briefly. 'Yes, sir.'

He lowered the musket. 'When?'

'Yesterday, sir.'

Just saying the words aloud made my anger spit like a fuse and I kicked a stone, hard, against the bark of a tree. When I looked up, he was watching me, though it wasn't the look of someone intent on harm. I took it to be a look of pity.

'Are you on foot?'

'No, sir, I got a horse.' I pointed back through the trees toward Samson. 'I caught the scent of yer fire but was afeared it might be Natives.'

He wagged his considerable chin toward the sky. 'It will soon be dark and this is not the hour to be alone in a forest.' I glimpsed a wall of sizable teeth. 'Go, fetch your horse, then come and warm yourself by the fire.'

'I'm much obliged, sir!'

With relief, I stumbled back through the brushwood and bracken and returned a few moments later with Samson. Slipping the fowler, horn and shot pouch over the saddle, I pulled the axe from my belt and pushed it in amongst the other items, but kept the knife to hand, after all, I knew nothing of this man except his deep voice sounded like the tide pulling shale from the shore.

Moving closer to the fire, I gratefully let the warmth seep into my cold bones. The man held out a hand the size of a shovel and announced, 'My name is Erik.'

'William, sir; William Baxter,' I answered, my fingers vanishing in his sizable palm.

'I have heard your accent many times. You hail from Ireland.'

'I do, sir. Where are you from?'

'I also come from across the sea. I am Dutch.'

I'd never heard of Dutch-land. Hoping to hide my ignorance, I changed the subject. 'Yer a fair size, sir. You got to be as big as a bear!'

His chuckle was like a rumble of thunder in a fur coat.

'How old are you, William?'

'Fourteen,' I replied, waiting for the full weight of his surprise, but he was kind enough to say nothing about my height.

Perching myself on a log by the fire, I watched as he cut the rabbit meat into fleshy chunks and threw them in an old pan on the embers where they sizzled and spat, browning in hot juices. Reaching into a leather bag, he lifted out several small apples, quartered them with his hunting knife, then dropped them into the pan along with some wild onions, a few silver-green leaves and a little water from his leather bottle.

'What leaves are they?' Ma never put leaves in stew.

'Sage. Have you never tasted sage?'

I told him we were not a family of leaf-eaters. I was also glad I had no appetite – I wouldn't have to eat the stew. To avoid further questions, I turned to admire Erik's horse. He was a beauty, his flanks glowing in the firelight. 'That's a fair big horse. Has he a name?'

'He is called Thor.'

It was a word I hadn't heard before, so assumed it was Dutch. 'You had him long?'

'About eight years.'

'Why isn't he tethered?'

'He does not like to be tied. I believe someone was cruel to him when he was young; tied and beat him. He must have suffered because he has scars on his flanks. When I first saw him, he was being sold as 'uncontrollable', but a little kindness solved that problem.'

'Is he not wilful? Doesn't he wander in the night?'

'No, he nibbles around the trees, but does not stray.'

Erik added a little more water to the stew as I studied the stallion. True enough, I could see the scars. Thor could flee if he had a mind to, yet chose to stay. That horse knows a good master, I decided.

Erik's voice broke into my thoughts, 'Do you want to tell me what happened to your folk?'

I was not ready to talk of the attack, not because I didn't want him to know, rather, I was afeared if I began talking, I wouldn't be able to stop. I was terrified the anger and hate would break like a hole in a beaver dam, and the trickle would become a torrent. I meant to reply, 'Thank you, but I prefer not to speak of it.' Instead, words I hadn't planned on saying tumbled from my lips as though someone had reached into my heart and hauled them out on a string.

'I was in the woods when Natives came over the creek. Da got everyone into the cabin, but...' The dam had broken. Streams of stinging water tumbled from my eyes. In a fit of anguish I cried, 'It was all my fault! I forgot to load the fowler! The Natives might have scattered if I'd fired a shot! I hate them! Someday I'll kill them like they killed my kin!'

Erik's deep, comforting voice rippled like a calm sea beside my crashing wrath, 'You must not blame yourself,' he soothed.

'You weren't there! You don't know!' I flung back at him. 'How will I survive without my kin! I'm completely alone!'

Burying my head in my knees, a storm of salty drops dripped on my boots. Erik let me cry. There were no fussing words. No advice on where I should go or what I should do. He just sat by the fire, stirring the stew until, at last, in halting, hiccoughing gasps, I raised my head and wiped the back of my hand across the snot running over my lips, feeling as worn out as an old shoe.

'William, tell me,' he asked gently, 'who do you look like, your mother or your father?'

'My ma,' I stammered. 'I've got her chestnut hair, and Da always said I've got her hands.' I spread out my filthy fingers and studied them as if somehow I might find Ma amongst the cuts and scrapes.

'Then remember this,' he continued, 'you carry these things from your mother wherever you go. That means you have her always with you.' He spoke the words as though they were the only thing in the whole world to be believed. 'Come now,' he added, 'try a little stew.' There was a kindness about him, a quiet strength that gave me heart.

'Reckon I harrowed up a great load of grief,' I mumbled, a little embarrassed.

'It is often the way, but it will help you recover.'

Tipping some stew into a wooden bowl, he handed it to me. I thought I might retch, but didn't want to be rude by refusing precious food. James would have sucked his own chops off for this meal. I sipped a little of the hot juice. To my surprise, it was very tasty. Dipping my fingers in the sauce, I lifted a tender morsel of meat and popped it in my mouth.

'Sage is not as bad as you thought?' he grinned.

A ghost of a smile crossed my lips, which was my second surprise. I thought I wouldn't smile for the rest of my life.

A gob of juice slid down my fingers and across the back of my hand, leaving a tiny furrow in the grime like a snail trail. I wiped it on my breeches as Erik speared a chunk of meat with his hunting knife and began to eat. For the first time, I wondered about his life and where he was heading. 'Do you live here?' It felt good to talk of something else.

'No, I only trap in this region. I am on my way north to a great river called the *Mahicanituck* – or the Hudson, as it is known in English. I trade there with a tribe called the Mahicans. I buy furs from them in exchange for knives, kettles and beads,' he pointed to his wares spread on the ground, 'then I sell the furs to traders returning to England, where there is a great demand for fur – especially fox.'

'Do the Mahican tribe number many?'

'They were a mighty nation until explorers and settlers arrived carrying disease, especially a sickness called smallpox. Now the Mahican are but a few hundred. There has been an outbreak of smallpox in Philadelphia this year, over one hundred people have died and they expect the disease to continue until spring.'

'How would I know if I had smallpox?'

He took a deep breath before replying, as though preparing for some great task. 'It begins with a fever and vomiting, which passes after a few days, then pus-filled blisters appear all over the body, even in the mouth and throat. It is important that no one touches the infected person because smallpox is so contagious that their bedding, clothes, and even the cabin must be burned. If there has been any contact with others, those folk must also be separated. You can see how a whole tribe can die from this one disease.'

'Is there no cure?'

'Well now, I will tell you something, William.' He laid his knife on the edge of the pot. 'The Natives who live north in New Scotland use a plant they say cures smallpox. It has one tall, dark red flower and the leaves are like a pitcher, they collect water. Flies and other insects fall in and drown and the plant eats them.'

'A plant that eats flies?' My teeth clenched.

'There is no proof the plant cures smallpox, but I have heard it from several sources.'

'Does it take long to die of smallpox?'

For a moment I thought he wasn't going to reply, then keeping his eyes fixed on the fire, he said quietly, 'It took six days for my wife to die.'

Shocked, I instantly regretted my words. 'I – I beg pardon. I ought to think before I speak.'

But Erik dismissed my apology with a flick of his hand, 'It was many years ago. I miss her still, of course, as you miss your folk, but I have survived the sorrow,' adding softly, 'and so will you.'

Again, a small smile tugged the edges of my lips. This man was dragging me slowly back to life as warmth draws an animal out of hibernation.

'Do you sell yer wares to other tribes?'

'Sometimes, but there are many tribes it is best to avoid. The most feared are the Haudenosaunee, known as the Iroquois by the French. Their home is many miles north. They are a powerful nation of six tribes and have conquered land as far south as the Delaware River. I hope you never meet them because they are indeed fearsome.'

As the fire died, we sat in comfortable silence finishing the meal. Gazing into the darkness, I wondered what would have become of me this night without the kindness of Erik. He had even coaxed me to take a little nourishment. As the moon rose higher, he lifted his gun and, assuring himself it was loaded, placed it by his side. Something about the weapon caught my eye. 'I have never seen a barrel of such a length!'

'Aha!' he exclaimed proudly. 'This gun is called a long rifle. They are a new design made by gunsmiths in Philadelphia. It is a little slower to load than a musket but very accurate. The long barrel means I can aim from about two hundred yards.' He handed it to me like a precious newborn baby. I ran my fingers along the barrel and over the smooth stock.

'Can I try it?'

'Indeed, but not tonight. It is late and we must rise early.'

Fetching a deerskin from the packhorse, he handed it to me, 'Here, wrap yourself in this. It will keep out the cold.'

I thanked him, then curled up and watched as he built up the fire with dry, broken branches, the hungry flames spitting sparks high into the darkness. There was a river of calmness in that big man's soul, and I reckon some of it splashed on me because my fear began to dwindle. I tried to stay awake, it's only polite to listen and make conversation as Da would have done, but my eyes were as heavy as rocks. I heard Erik mention an old Native path that went toward Philadelphia, then he paused to fill his pipe with a spit of baccy, and in that moment, I dreamed myself safely back in the cabin and Ma at my side kissing me goodnight.

THE BEAR

'Look lively, boy!'

Erik's voice broke into my dreamless sleep. Rolling over, I stretched, then threw off the deerskin and clambered unsteadily to my feet. Dawn had already gripped the horizon and was now climbing over the hills. While Erik fetched wood, I scraped dry moss from the side of a tree, scooped up handfuls of old, brown pine needles, placed them on the still glowing embers, then blew gently until a low flame burst into life. Erik returned with an armful of dry branches and before long that fire was melting the frost around our feet.

Until the rabbit stew of the previous night, I had never before seen a man prepare food. Da simply sat at the table and waited for the food to come to him. But Erik now produced a small bag of flour from his satchel, tipped some into a bowl, then mixed it with a handful of warm water from the pot on the fire. Kneading the paste until it was flat and smooth, he then placed it on a hot stone in the flames.

'While the bread is cooking, we will pull some cattails because there is no more meat. Do you know where to find cattails?' I looked at him blankly, which was becoming a habit because there was much I didn't understand. 'Come,' he encouraged, 'I will show you.'

Walking a little way through the trees, we slithered down a slope of frosty leaves to the edge of a small stream. 'Cattails grow on marshland, or by rivers,' he explained, 'they are a good source of food when there is little else to eat. There,' he pointed, 'those are cattails.'

The frozen plants looked more dead than alive to me, their long, icy stems folded like the legs of a dead spider. Kneeling on broken bits of old bark to keep his knees dry, Erik pushed up his sleeve and plunged a hand down into the cold, boggy ground. 'Work the plant free of mud – then give a gentle pull,' he explained. There was a squelching plop, and he held up what looked like a jumble of muddy worms. 'Tonight, we will scrape the skins and cook the roots over the fire.' He was a good and patient teacher, and I was beginning to understand there was plenty of food around if only I knew where to look for it.

By the time we returned to the fire, the bread was blistered and black. 'Ah, just the way I like it!' he grinned. Flipping it from hand to hand to cool it, he then tore the bread in half and generously offered me a piece, which I gratefully accepted. Settled again by the fire, I turned my mind to the long journey ahead of me. It had done me good to have company, in fact so much good, that I had no desire to strike out again alone. The fears of yesterday were returning; how would I find my way? Would I be attacked by Natives? Where would I sleep? Trying to hide my mounting unease, I asked, 'Is the path to Philadelphia far from here?'

'A short distance, but as it happens, I also journey that way.'

I stared at him in surprise. 'You will travel with me?'

'There is no reason why we should not ride together,' he shrugged.

I slumped with relief. The knot in my chest eased, and I realised I'd been rigid as a rock with dread. 'I'm right grateful for yer company,' I mumbled, with more gratitude than I had words to express. This time I wouldn't be travelling alone in miles of fearful forest. For a few days at least, I would be safe. I thought again on my good fortune, not only had I spent a night in safety, but now I would have the protection of this giant.

Erik reached into his pocket and took out a scrap of folded cloth. Inside were six small, dark, lumpy cakes. With a *snap*, he broke one of the cakes in half, dropped it in his old pewter mug, added some warm water and began to stir it with his knife. The smell was peculiar, not unlike the coffee house. Aware of my wide-eyed interest, he offered me a taste, 'Here – have a sip. It is called chocolate. I buy it in New York.'

I put the hot, dark liquid to my lips. It lay rich and smooth on my tongue then slid slowly down my gullet. It tasted so divine I wondered if it might be one of those sins Reverend Bertram warned us about, because if it was – I wanted more.

'Could I buy that in Philadelphia?'

'If you have the money!' he chortled. 'Chocolate is costly, but when I have sold my skins, I always buy a quarter-pound. It is a hot drink on a cold morning.'

He poured some of the steaming liquid into a bowl for me, and there we sat, sipping warm chocolate in the quiet, early morning mist.

Before the sun had topped the trees, we were on our way to the town of Lancaster. The riding was hard, but Samson clomped steadily behind the packhorse along a trail that ran through the forest like an old brown snake. We had been riding for most of the morning when dark clouds began gobbling up the smudges of blue sky, and I could feel what Ma called 'a brawling wind looking for a fight'! It slammed into my back, wrestled the trees, then hurled rain down upon us with all the force of a mill wheel shot.

'We must find shelter!' shouted Erik.

The snoring of a giant troll rumbled across the sky. Samson whinnied and veered from the path in terror.

'He's afeared of thunder!' I cried. Jumping down, I pulled off my neckerchief and tied it over his eyes.

'There is a cave ahead! Follow me!' bellowed Erik.

Tugging Samson through the flying leaves and stinging rain, I followed Erik to a stony cave in the hillside where brown bats hung high in the roof crevices, and black droppings lay in piles below their roost. Samson trotted gratefully undercover along with the packhorse, then I ran again into the gale to help with Thor.

'I will gather wood for a fire!' shouted Erik above the thunder, his large feet slapping away through the slushy mud. I grabbed Thor's reins, but he began to stamp and pull. 'Ho, boy!' I pleaded, but he reared and snorted until he had ripped the reins right out of my wet fingers and all I could see was his rump disappearing through the trees. I threw up my hands in frustration; damn horse!

A dark shadow suddenly crossed over me. I sensed a looming presence. There was something behind me. Something that reeked like a wet buck. My heart stumbled. My legs turned to quicksand – my lungs to bags of flour. Dumb with dread, I swung toward the danger. A bear. Large. Black. Instinct screamed – run! *Run!* But there was no escape right or left. A huge, daggered paw ripped through my cheek, sending me tumbling like a rag doll. There was no pain, only shock. Blood pulsed down my face. It ran into my mouth. The taste of old coins. I squirmed in the mud, frantically trying to wriggle away from the beast. A scream – my scream – rose on the wind. With all the power of an ocean, the bear surged toward me like one giant, frothing, black wave. I curled, bracing myself against teeth and claws.

Time was suddenly hauled backward by its breeches. Everything slowed. Movement flashed at the corner of my eye. Something reared. Reins flailed in the wind. Thor! He bucked. Two strong back legs smashed into the bear's shoulder. The beast lost balance. It was all the time I needed. Stumbling to my feet I started running, hurdling through the undergrowth. I glanced behind – the bear was chasing, gaining with every stride, powerful muscles rippling beneath its thick, black fur.

A booming cry rose above the storm, 'Get down! *Down!*'

I flung myself onto the drenched earth – my face buried in chinquapin burs. Lungs bursting. Heart beating like a jig gone mad.

A shot split the hammering rain. I lay motionless, eyes wildly searching – where was the bear? Gone? Dead? Suddenly, half a ton of flesh and fur crashed down on top of me, crushing my ribs and forcing the air from my lungs. I frantically tried to inhale, to wriggle out from under the weight, but I was trapped.

Erik hurried to my side. Wrapping his strong arms around the beast, he tried to haul the enormous bulk from my body, but the bear was too heavy even for him. Blood pumped hard in my head. Alarm gripped Erik's face. He whistled; a high, loud, shrill sound that could be heard even above the rain. It brought Thor to his side. Grabbing a rope from the saddle, he threw the looped end over Thor's neck, then knotted the other end around the bear's legs and began to force the horse backwards.

'Trekken! Trekken! Pull!'

Thor snorted, stamped his hooves and heaved until, inch by inch, the hulking body of that bear began to move, releasing me from suffocation. Sweet, damp air flew down my throat, but my relief turned to excruciating pain. 'My chest!' I gasped.

Erik swept me up as though I weighed no more than a feather, carried me into the cave, and lowered me gently onto the cold, stony ground. Fetching skins and pelts from the packhorse, he quickly made a bed toward the back wall, away from the wind and rain, where I lay shivering with cold and shock. He then retrieved the firewood, wrenched a bundle of dry moss from the entrance of the cave, and before long flames were casting flickering shadows across the walls.

'William, try not to move. I believe you have broken ribs. I will bind your chest, but first, I must cut off your jacket as it is soaked with rain and blood.' With the precision of a butcher, he slid his hunting knife the length of my coat and around the shoulder seams, then removed it in bloody shreds. Fetching the blue trading cloth from the packhorse, he then wound a long strip tightly around my chest, which eased my breathing. 'Fortunately, your shirt and breeches are only a little damp and will dry. Now, I will tend to your face.' Tipping water from his leather bottle onto a piece of clean cloth, he gently bathed the wound, wiping away the grit and mud. The feeling in my cheek was slowly returning, and a searing pain now stretched all the way from my chin to my forehead.

'The skin has been ripped open the full length of your cheek – all the way to your chin,' he sighed. 'Fortunately it is a clean slice, but cannot be left like that. It will have to be stitched.'

Stitched! My courage buckled at the thought. 'No, *no*! Can't you bandage it?' Erik shook his head and I could see he was not looking forward to this any more than me.

'Be brave, my young friend. I will work quickly.'

'Now?' I whimpered.

'*Ja.*' He nodded, reaching for his bag. 'The sooner I begin the sooner it will be finished. Rum would help the pain, but I do not carry alcohol because there are Natives who would kill me for it. I am sorry.'

'It's not your fault,' I mumbled.

Rummaging inside his leather bag, he produced a bone needle almost the length of his hand. The sight of it sent the cave walls spinning, but Erik was muttering again in Dutch. It seemed when things weren't going well he preferred his own language. '*Ik heb geen draad.*' He sighed. 'I have no thread.'

'Would rabbit sinew do?' I ventured. I had enough sinew to stitch an army. 'It's in a bag on my saddle.'

I can't say he smiled – it wasn't the time for smiling, but he could see I was resigned to the situation and trying to help. While he threaded the needle, I lay flat, shoved my hands under my thighs and screwed up my eyes tight as a trap. I felt him pinch the two sides together with his fingers, then he pushed the needle through the skin.

I screamed! I kicked! I twisted and punched his arm! The pain couldn't have been more excruciating if a red-hot poker had been forced against my face! He continued, pulling the needle quickly through the other flap of skin as I fought for breath, my aching ribs throbbing with every heave of my chest. Dragging the two sides of the wound together, he knotted the sinew.

'The first stitch is finished,' he encouraged. The first! How many more would I have to endure! Waiting until my breathing calmed, he began the second stitch. This time the walls of the cave swam in circles around my head. My arms lost all strength, and just when I thought I was going to vomit, darkness rose up and smothered me.

A flutter of firelight wriggled under my lashes. My cheek was on fire and my chest had surely been bashed with a hammer. Glancing toward the mouth of the cave, I could see twinkling lights hanging from a dark sky.

'Ah, the warrior has returned!' smiled Erik. Rising from the fireside, he placed an arm under my head and tipped a few cool drops of water into my mouth. 'Well, young William, you have eight stitches. *Ja!*' He nodded, seeing my surprise. 'Fortunately, you were not awake!'

But I was feeling more than pain. I felt unwell; shivery. Pulling the beaver skin up to my neck, my gaze fell on something large and black standing in the shadows not five yards from me. I gripped the pelt. Had Erik not seen the danger? A gust of wind suddenly filled the cave. The shadow moved! I was on my feet in an instant, screeching with fright.

'Do not be alarmed, William!' Arms wide, Erik barred my escape. 'It is only the *bearskin* hanging on the wall to dry!'

I looked again at the listless, dark shadow. 'You hinned huh hair?' I couldn't have slobbered more if a barber-surgeon had just pulled my tooth.

'Of course I skinned the bear – it will fetch a good price.'

'I hought hair attacks were rare?'

'Bear attacks *are* rare, but I believe it had chosen this place to hibernate and was angry at finding us here. I had no choice but to shoot it, otherwise, it would have killed you.'

Picking up a pile of skins, he sat against the wall of the cave with the needle and sinew and began to sew. 'Since your coat is ruined, I am making you a new one.'

I lay watching Erik's fingers work steadily by the light of the fire. His large hands were surprisingly nimble with a needle. It was obvious this wasn't the first time he'd made a coat. Outside, the storm was bending boughs and hurling leaves like scarlet snow into the cave where they hissed and curled in the flames.

'Sleep now,' murmured Erik, 'and you will soon recover.'

I slept, but I did not recover. Heat engulfed me. Kicking away the pelt, I rolled onto the cold stones. Time meant nothing. I had no care if it was day or night. Sometimes I felt water on my cheek and Erik's hand gently cleaning the wound, then the cave walls whirled into forested hills. I was on the ridge above the settlement. Painted men were hauling themselves up over the edge, trying to grab my legs. I thrashed and kicked! Desperately I tried to load the fowler, but the powder horn fell from my hands again and again, until I was on my knees weeping in a puddle of black dust.

Birdsong. I could hear the tee-tee-sip of the snow buntings and the warbling of winter finches. The roaring furnace inside my body had died. Jagged stone walls welcomed my return, and I found my face swaddled like an infant; a cloth tied around my head and knotted under my chin. I must have looked like Grandma in her headscarf.

'William!' Relief flooded across Erik's face. Kneeling beside me, he laid a hand on my forehead. 'The fever has passed. The maggots have saved your life.'

'Haggots?'

He nodded. 'Three days have passed since I placed them on your wound. They have eaten all the rotting flesh and infection.' Unwinding the cloth from my head, he lifted the creatures from my cheek. Six, creamy, plump maggots wriggled in the palm of his hand. 'All living things have their purpose,' he stated, grinning.

By evening the pain in my cheek had improved to a dull ache, but now my guts were rumbling. I hadn't eaten for three days and the mouth-watering smell of cooking meat, sage and apple now filled the cave.

'Bear stew!' exclaimed Erik happily. 'Do you want to try a little meat? Chewing will hurt,' he warned.

One look at my eager expression settled the matter.

The meat tasted much like deer, but sweeter. I chewed slowly, dribbling splotches down my shirt like a bairn and sucking up the sauce with a noisy slurp, for I could use but one side of my mouth. Erik, meanwhile, bayoneted morsels of meat with his knife and chewed contentedly. When he had finally demolished a meal that would have lasted me a week, he built up the fire, slumped down against the wall of the cave and was soon softly snoring. I reckon he hadn't slept for days.

Shuffling to the mouth of the cave, I surveyed the damage. High above the battered branches, a calm, dusky heaven slowly darkened from cornflower blue to deep violet, sprinkled with a wash of silver drops. It was my turn to keep watch. Determined to rise to the responsibility, I sat by the fire and loaded the fowler, as bats skimmed my hair and disappeared into the twilight. I was armed and ready for any danger. Completely prepared. Erik could count on me.

Within minutes, sleep felled me like an axe.

Four more days passed before I was truly recovered and able to continue our journey. By then, Erik said I looked like a bare-knuckle boxer; the right side of my bruised, swollen face now a mix of green, yellow and purple. I punched him on the arm to prove him right, a knock that would have made any other man take a step backwards, but Erik didn't move an inch. I doubt he even felt it.

My new coat was finished. The King of England himself had surely never owned such a fine garment. Erik had used a mix of beaver, deer and wolf skins; two down each front, one in the making of each sleeve, two large skins for the back and a small beaver pelt formed the hood. I earnestly thanked that good man, slipped my arms into the soft sleeves and fastened it with Da's belt. My old wool jacket had been heavy and scratched my neck, but this coat was as light and soft as a blanket of blossom. It would be true to say, however, it was a mite too large; it came right down over my boots and I had to roll back the cuffs. Erik said I would grow into it. I hoped never to grow out of it.

I was glad to leave the cave. Coming so close to death had made me realise how much I wanted to live. For the first time since losing my kin, I felt myself rising from my grief, suddenly hungry for life. Outside, a heavy frost had settled during the night and frozen leaves cracked beneath my boots. Fresh, cold air tugged my ears and nipped my nose, and tiny ice needles fluffed the shrubs. It was so pleasing; a glorious sight. A gift. A sparkling welcome back to the world, just for me.

THE SLAVE

The trail turned inland and that world of light and sparkle disappeared as we entered the domain of the dead. In that thick forest, neither sound nor sunlight broke through the still, damp air. Drooping, dripping branches hung like the outstretched arms of a sorcerer, silently waiting to snatch a young boy. I was thankful I wasn't alone in that murky, desolate place.

We crossed a small river Erik called Conoy Creek, but as the day wore on my ribs and face began to ache and I began to wilt in the saddle. Erik must have seen I was struggling because he kindly said we'd find some refreshment and rest for the night in the next village. I was rightly relieved and thinking on a bowl of hot food when a sudden rumbling behind made us both turn and peer backward along the path. A band of men on horseback were thundering toward us, their wide-eyed horses hurling misty, silver breath into the cold air.

'Under the trees!' cried Erik.

I gave poor Samson such a kick in the ribs he moved right smartly, just in time to avoid calamity as the riders galloped past; whipping their sweating steeds and leaving us in a whirl of leaves and hurtling mud.

'Fools!' bristled Erik.

'Why were they riding at such a speed?'

'I cannot say, but they could have killed us!' he seethed.

At last, that dread forest gave way to sunlight and open fields of rich, dark soil where maize had been harvested: the frozen stubble spiking toward the sky. Soon we found ourselves in a busy village, the surge of heat from a glowing blacksmith's fire warming us as we rode past. In sturdy boots and leather apron, the sweating, muscled man pounded a red-hot horseshoe then lowered it into a bucket of water where it hissed in a cloud of steam. A little further on, a large board on the side of the road read, 'John Galbraith. Flour and Sawmill', but this was nothing to my astonishment when I heard the voices of the people, 'Erik! These folk are from my homeland!'

'That is no surprise because this village is called Donegal. I believe there is such a place in Ireland?'

'Donegal is but a three-day walk from my home!'

I hadn't expected to be among my own kind again until I was on Irish soil, but as I listened to all their speak, I could have been happily walking the road to Banagher!

I was suddenly slapped from my fancies by loud, desperate cries. The sound was coming from the sawmill. Four men, the very same who had sped past us along the trail, were hauling a man, a slave, from his hiding place behind a pile of logs. Kicks and blows rained down upon him until he spat blood from swollen, crimson lips. I watched, horrified, as he was tossed to the ground at the feet of a short, stout, greasy-haired man with a belly that bulged over his breeches and a fat, pimpled neck that oozed over his collar.

'Well na! You've led me a merry dance all the way from Williamsburg!' The man stopped to draw breath, sucking in air with a wheeze, the veins on his nose flowing like tiny red rivers toward the tip of his bulbous snout. 'An' you will not escape a third time! String 'im up, boys!' he snarled. 'Show 'im what happens to runaways!'

I knew not until that day, what a pitiful thing it is to hear a man beg for his life.

'No! Massa, *no!*' His cries near turned my guts.

Binding his wrists, they threw a rope over a high branch and hauled the slave from the ground where he twisted and turned, his head hanging so far backward his terrified eyes could see only the sky. A small crowd gathered as the fat man unhooked a coiled cartwhip from his saddle and cracked it out as though he was practising.

'Na, boy, I told you if you eva run away agin, I would whip yaw hide t' death, and that is what I am gonna do!' he growled, jerking the whip backward through the air.

Lash!

Now, my da had belted me from time to time and I'd considered myself rightly hard done by, but I had never witnessed anything like that whipping. The slave howled. His grimy shirt shredded. I could see old wounds – his back had already been flogged like a furrowed field by some previous punishment. This new torture reopened the old scars. Ribbons of blood ran down his legs, dripping from his toes to the cold earth.

Lash!

I gaped at the sight in horror. 'Erik, they can't really mean to kill him?'

'Slaves have no rights, William,' he answered flatly. 'That fat man is an overseer and can punish the slave as he pleases.'

Lash!

'Is there nothing we can do?'

He stared at me in dismay. 'You think we should meddle in this? There is a fine of thirty shillings for anyone helping a slave to escape!'

I cared not a biting-bug if there was a fine of thirty shillings.

'Erik, can't we cut him down and steal him away from here?' I continued, expecting a good scolding for even thinking such a thing, but Erik was fingering his chin stubble, deep in thought, so I tried to be patient and keep my gob shut.

Lash!

Finally, he glanced around to make certain no one was listening, then leaned toward me and whispered, 'William, I have a friend who works in a tavern in Lancaster. This friend knows a Quaker family who offer shelter to runaway slaves. If the slave survives, I will take him to the tavern. From there, my friend will guide me to the safety of the Quaker house. This could mean great danger. You must not feel obliged to help, for if I am caught, I may be hanged. That is the punishment for stealing another man's property.'

'Hanged?' I blurted.

'Ssh!' He patted the air. 'Do you want the whole village to hear?' Yet even as he voiced that terrifying truth, not once did he flinch from the task he had set himself. His eyes remained steadfast on mine, determined and fearless, whereas I asked the only question a fourteen-year-old would ask, 'Will I be hanged?'

'Fortunately, you are small. You could claim to be about ten years of age. You may receive a flogging, but I have never heard of anyone as young as ten being hanged.' He paused, allowing time for this information to register. 'It will also mean riding through the night. Will your face and ribs stand another five hours in the saddle?'

Erik was about to risk his freedom, possibly even his life, for a slave. This was surely a lesson in the true meaning of charity. It flowed from him like a waterfall. He was a cascade of compassion dressed in fur. I cringed as the slave's body swung helplessly with each lash. My injuries were nothing compared to his suffering. Even if my ribs and cheek throbbed for the entire journey and I finished with a flogging, I would never again gripe about pain, not as long as I lived.

'If you are willing to risk yer life, Erik, I can risk a flogging,' I answered, determined to help.

Beckoning me along the road toward a huddle of towering trees, we dismounted under spiky, pine-scented branches to bide our time. I made a cushion of dry pine needles to keep my rump off the cold earth and settled down. Before long it seemed even the old sun could no longer watch, because it slowly dipped its face and slid behind the hills.

The agonising groans of the slave fell silent at last. Only then did that murderous overseer roll up his bloody whip and swagger with his men to the tavern; a two-story building sitting side-on to the road only twenty yards from our hiding place. When the door swung open, we could glimpse inside, and it was during one of these moments we heard the overseer announce he was going to buy drinks for the whole tavern to celebrate the capture of his slave! *Celebrate!* I knew he had every right to whip the slave – but to celebrate the deed? How could anyone raise a glass to such cruelty? With ease, it seemed, because raucous cheering immediately erupted and folk banged their empty mugs on the tables in appreciation! I wanted to spit in their ale, or better still – pee in it.

Now, in any place the Irish gather there will be singing. They begin with the good old songs; clapping, tapping their feet and having a rare old time. But by the wee, small hours, they're singing all the sorrowful laments they can remember, weeping into their ale for the state of Ireland and promising to love each other forever. At least, any wake, wedding, or wetting of heads that I'd ever attended had been like that.

As the hours passed, strains of *Fare Thee Well Fine Lady* drifted across the road:

'*Walking down Tanner's Lane, so I've been told*
'*He met a fine lady who offered him gold.*'

It was an old song; I knew it well, but I wasn't in the mood for singing.

Silently, we continued to wait. Folk crowded into the tavern as though it was a Wake and food was expected. In cabins all along the street, candlelight glimmered through cracked, wooden doors, reminding me of home, but it didn't sadden me. Instead, I thought of all the unfortunate slaves and the suffering they endured, and while it was a tragedy to lose my kin, the lives of those poor slaves were wretched from beginning to end.

The full moon ambled higher, hanging above us like a huge, silver shilling. My feet were cold and my muscles cramped. I glanced at Erik and whispered, 'How much longer?'

'Soon,' he mouthed, 'be patient.'

As though the innkeeper had heard us, the tavern door was suddenly flung open, and the entire company staggered out into the frosty air – the overseer, his men and a whole gaggle of villagers. Still singing, they lurched down the road like sailors in a heavy swell, their merrymaking finally fading into the night, while in the tavern, a ring of soft candlelight drifted up past the stair window, and moments later, the building was in darkness.

Silence blanketed the village, broken only by the ghostly grunts of bucks in the rut across the fields. Cautiously, Erik and I crept through the undergrowth toward the hanging man. His bloody body was covered in a sickening mix of fresh and old scars. Several fingers on his right hand had been severed. My guts churned at the thought of how that had been achieved. Finally, Erik shook his head; the slave was dead. I knew not what to think. Perhaps it was better this way; his trials and pain were at an end.

Now, Da had always told me I was clumsy. He said I couldn't carry a tune without falling over, and as it happened, I chose that precise moment to prove him right. As I turned back toward the horses, my foot slipped on a frosty branch and a loud *crack* resounded in the still, night air. Instinct forced us low. I grimaced at Erik in alarm, but he didn't reply. He was gazing up at a pair of wide, desperate, brown eyes. The eyes of the slave. He was alive!

'William!' Erik whispered. 'Bring some water and a deerskin from the packhorse. Make haste, boy!'

Darting back to the horses, I unhooked my leather bottle, slung it over my shoulder, then pulled a deerskin from Erik's roll of pelts. When I returned, Erik had already lowered the slave from the tree and slit the rope binding his wrists. The poor man gulped from the bottle as though he hadn't had water for a week. Carefully, we wrapped him in the deerskin, then Erik carried him to the waiting horses and we were out of the village in a trice, leaving no hoof-prints or trace of our mischief because the frosted ground was as hard as a blacksmith's hammer.

It would take us most of the night to reach Lancaster, and I had only one regret: I wouldn't be there to witness the overseer's rage in the morning and hoped he would suffer a seizure and die.

MAGGIE

In the ghostly moonlight, the amber eyes of a fox crossed our path. Hunched turkeys roosted in the branches above our heads, their feathered forms silhouetted against the shining orb. Mice and voles scuttled under leaves, hiding from the silent swoop of an owl. From a high rock, the steady, green eyeshine of a mountain lion followed our every move. Erik placed a finger on the trigger-guard of his rifle and kept his eyes on the beast.

I found if I straightened my back and puffed out my chest, I could breathe more easily, and even though my cheek was smarting like a good slap, I held fast to my promise; not once in those dark hills did I complain of pain.

At last, we arrived at Lancaster. To my surprise, this small town was no jumble of wooden cabins like Donegal. Tall, brick houses bordered the streets, row upon row, silent as sleeping sentries as we passed in the shadows. Coming to a large square, we stopped beside a horse trough where the icy water glinted with frost. Erik surveyed the slumbering streets to get his bearings, then with a nod of his head, whispered, 'This way.' Urging Samson onward, I followed Thor across the square to a row of houses called King Street, where Erik pointed to a painted sign outside a two-story lodge: The Hickory Tree Tavern. We had arrived.

Urging the horses to the rear of the lodge, we came to a small yard where the light from an oil lamp cast an arc over a three-bay wooden barn. The first bay was stacked almost to the roof with barley straw, the second housed a small cart, and in the third bay stood a grey horse that gazed at us with large, startled eyes. Across the yard, a rickety outhouse had been stocked with firewood – the outhouse itself slumped in such poor repair I reckoned one good gust might tumble it. Nearby, a brick well with a bucket hanging on a rope, signalled where to find water for the horses.

At Erik's bidding, I slid to the ground, tethered Samson and the packhorse to one of the barn posts and tiptoed over to the large, black, tavern door.

'Ask for Maggie,' mouthed Erik.

I knocked as loudly as I dared, hoping Maggie, whoever she was, would rouse herself with a bit more haste on account of my frozen feet. A light fog had descended and misty goblin breath began to swirl about us, fingering my face and giving me the frights. I am not a lover of fog – afeared something I cannot see might be watching me.

As there was no answer to my first tentative tap on the door, I knocked a second time. Almost immediately there was the squeak of a bolt and the door creaked open, throwing a slice of light on the frosty ground. A young woman, carrying a candle and wearing a nightgown and shawl, stared at me.

'Pray, excuse us at this late hour, madam—'

They were the only words I had time to say. Her eyes suddenly widened with surprise and she ran past me into the yard, her thick, auburn hair flowing like a flame. 'Dutch!'

I stood dumbfounded by the door. I hadn't expected Maggie to be so, um, beautiful.

Holding the slave steady, Erik reached down with one arm, girdled her waist and lifted her off the ground, whereupon she threw her arms around his neck, and when she had finally bestowed half a dozen kisses on him, asked, 'What brings you here at this hour?'

I decided they knew each other.

'Maggie, we have a badly whipped slave,' Erik whispered, nodding to the bundle in his arms. 'Can you direct us to the Quaker house?'

That good woman lifted the corner of the deerskin, and her happy expression faded. 'Who is responsible for this?'

'The overseer, the slave is a runaway.'

'You won't find your way in the dark. I'll take you there. This fog is a blessing; it will help conceal us, but if we are separated, follow the road across the market square toward Wright's Ferry.' She hastily disappeared back into the tavern for coat and boots, as the slave, who had slept the entire journey, awoke with the sound of their voices.

'What is your name?' Erik's voice was calm and reassuring.

'Jacob, sir.'

'We are taking you to a house of safety, Jacob. They will hide you until your wounds have healed, then good employment will be found for you.'

'God bless you for your kineness, sir, or I be dead for sure. Ma Massa, he a crazy man. If I hang the baccy in the dryin' barn, he whip me. If I takin' the hog heads downriver, he whip me. He whip me no madda whad I do.'

He fell silent again as Maggie reappeared now with a long, black cape over her nightgown and wearing knee-length boots. Leading the horse from the barn, she swung herself upon its bare back and beckoned us toward the lane. Leaving the packhorse tethered, we followed her across the silent market square, continuing toward Wright's Ferry until she halted by a low stone wall. I could see no dwelling of any kind, but Maggie jumped to the ground and, feeling her way along the wall, melted into the darkness. Erik slid to the ground with the slave in his arms, but as he waited for Maggie's signal, Jacob grabbed the collar of his coat and blurted in panic, 'If he fine you, sir, he kill you!'

'Have no fear for our safety,' assured Erik, 'we will be on our guard.'

In the distance, the small halo of a lighted candle told us Maggie had woken those kind, courageous folk, and a moment later we heard her soft voice calling Erik to bring the slave.

'God bless you, Jacob,' I whispered. He briefly clutched my hand, then Erik swept him away toward the light, leaving me alone in the dark with only the horses.

Fog snaked around me. Its chill, damp claws circled my body. The trees began to creak as though they were moving closer. Leaves rustled with laughter. Bony fingered branches pointed toward me. 'Catch the boy!' they cackled. 'Seize him!' Tree roots curled around my ankles. They slithered up my legs and twisted around my waist, pinning my arms to my sides! They coiled up around my neck!

Maggie and Erik suddenly loomed out of the darkness, and I don't mind saying I was never so glad in all my life to have their company.

We arrived back at the tavern as dawn fanned across the sky like the tail feathers of a peacock. Now, it was not usual for me to pay attention to such a thing, but that morning was unlike any other morning. I had helped save a life, and that made *my* life worth something.

Erik carried the pelts inside while I stabled the horses, giving them fresh water from the well and plenty of good barley straw. By the time I'd finished, the first sounds of life were drifting toward us from the town. Maggie closed the door, drove home that big iron bolt, then grabbed my arm and took a turn with me around the floor, the two of us downright giddy with elation! I had never seen anyone so lovely. Her face was a field of freckles, her eyes emerald green, and every strand of her thick, wavy hair, the colour of autumn apples.

It would be fair to say the place reeked of stale beer. The beamed ceiling hung butter-yellow from years of pipe and wood smoke, while above the fire, a large, heavy pot hung on a chain; the black, crusted rim glinting in the early light streaming through the front window. Behind a scratched, pitted, wooden counter, casks were stacked five high against a wall. Tables and chairs stood about the place, several piled with pewter plates and mugs, all waiting for customers. Near the heavy back door by which we had entered, stairs black as ebony curled to an upper floor, the middle of each step worn shiny from years of countless boots.

Erik coaxed the fire back to life, slumped in a stick-backed chair – the squeaky legs protesting under his weight – pulled off his boots and wriggled his toes by the flames. Meanwhile, Maggie disappeared into the back scullery and reappeared with three small trout, slapped them on a griddle with some sliced potatoes, and laid them on the embers.

The tantalising smell of frying fish and hot grease gradually filled the room, and when Maggie placed hot potatoes, flatbread and fish before me, I greedily mopped up every morsel. Erik explained how he and I had met and of the bear attack. Maggie leaned over, brushed the hair from my cheek and gently laid her long fingers on my wounded face. It was like the touch of an angel.

'Now, up those stairs!' she gave me a gentle push, 'I have a meal to prepare, or my customers will complain!'

I followed her upstairs to a small, sparsely furnished chamber. The room was cold, I could see my own breath, but it was not as cold as the forest. A large, straw-filled sack, supported by ropes tied across a rough, wooden frame on legs, served as a bed. On top of the sack lay a grey woollen blanket, while beside the bed, a jug of water, an earthen bowl and a folded square of clean linen sat on a small table, inviting the guest to rid himself of the day's dust. Crossing to a small window, I nudged aside the heavy, green drape and gazed down upon the road. Folk dressed in heavy woollen garments now hurried along the street. Metal-rimmed cartwheels crunched and slid on icy patches, while across the square, children bashed frozen shards of water from the horse trough.

Kicking off my boots, I spread the blanket on the sacking and crawled beneath it – stretching my back to ease my ribs. In the next chamber, I could hear Erik and Maggie quietly talking. It reminded me of Ma and Da whispering under the porch when they thought we were asleep, and I reckoned I could become rightly fond of this place.

THE OVERSEER

Someone was prodding me.

'William! *William!*' the voice sounded urgent.

Startled from my slumber, I rolled over and squinted against the light. Erik was standing by the bed.

'What is the hour?' I mumbled.

'It is midday but…' He had no need to say more. From outside I heard a voice we both knew well, and my blood congealed at the sound.

'Na, listen here! Somebody stole one o' ma slaves, an' I am gonna find out who is responsible for this wicked deed!' demanded the angry overseer.

Wicked deed? He could hardly speak of wicked deeds! Scrambling from the sack, I pushed back the drape, rubbed the wet glass with a squeaky wipe of my fingers and peered down at the road. A small crowd had gathered around a fat man who was spitting with fury.

'Na, I am lookin' fow two particula' fellas: a large man an' a small boy. If anyone here has information about these fellas, I will pay handsomely. They were seen by me an' my men in the village where ma slave disappeared.' He spat out a lump of chewed baccy covered in thick, yellow saliva, then pointed a short, fat finger to the sky like a possessed prophet. 'Nobody makes a fool outta me! Ya hear? *Nobody!* Men! Start with this here tavern!'

I stared at Erik. 'It isn't possible! No one saw us rescue Jacob!'

Erik quickly headed for the chamber door. 'I will go down and face them. It is better than hiding up here like a rat in a hole.'

'Wait!' I insisted. He stopped mid-stride. 'Even if they can't prove it, they could beat you badly on suspicion of the deed, but they won't harm a lad as small as me. I'll tell them you left at dawn – that we journeyed together for only a short while.'

'I cannot leave you to face the overseer alone!' he argued.

'William is right.' Erik whirled around. Maggie stood in the doorway. 'You best get out of here, Dutch. There's a narrow path behind the barn. It runs along the back of this street and will take you to the forest. Leave the packhorse, but take Thor or they will know you haven't gone far. When it's safe, I will come for you.' Still, Erik hesitated. 'I'll stay with William, I promise,' she assured, 'now go!'

Speeding through the doorway, Erik leapt right over the stair rail, dropped to the floor below and disappeared by the back door. Maggie also descended, her tread on each step as graceful as a timid deer. I took a deep breath to calm my churning guts. The Reverend Bertram said lying was a sin, but I was doing it to save Jacob from being discovered, the good Quaker folk from being punished, and Erik from having the beating of his life.

Below stairs, the tavern was all noise and bustle. Folk were supping, drinking and playing cards and table games. One of the overseer's men stepped inside and immediately laid his evil eyes on me.

'The boy is here!' he crowed. 'Here in the tavern!'

A few moments later, the overseer himself waddled across the threshold, his piggy eyes glinting with triumph at finding at least one of us. Behind him tumbled the rest of his men, while I sauntered over to the fire and leaned against the wall as though taking my ease.

Maggie bent over a pot of stew, stirring it with a ladle as if she hadn't a care in the world.

'Na I have you!' The odour of sour, old sweat seeped from his plump flesh. 'Where is yaw fether?' he demanded.

'Good day to you, sir,' said I, as though I had never before set eyes upon him. 'My da? My da is dead.' This at least was true.

One of his henchmen piped up, 'We wanna speak to the man who was with you! Where is he?'

'If youse are talking of the big man, he took his leave early this morning.'

The overseer slammed a fist on the nearest table, making the empty mugs jump and every voice hush. 'I don't wanna speak to no boy!' he shouted in angry frustration.

'You got no choice, mister!' I answered squarely. The insolence of me! I even surprised myself.

'You have a ready tongue, young man!' he barked. 'Now wad d'you know about ma slave?'

I folded my arms. 'I don't know nothing about yer slave.'

'You *stole* him from Donegal!' He suddenly wagged the finger at me as Ma used to do. I briefly wondered if we were related.

'We took no slave, sir. We *were* in Donegal, and I mind now the slave you're speaking of – he was hanging from a tree?'

'You know he was, damnable boy!' he blustered.

'I can assure you, sir, we continued on to Lancaster, arriving here at sunset.'

He studied me, his face fermenting. I held steady. There was only one person moving, and that was Maggie, tending to her work.

Like a predator slowly advancing for the kill, the overseer moved toward me. 'That slave is hidin' in this tavern, an' I am gonna' find him! Above stairs!' he shouted to his men. 'Search the chambers!'

They bounded up the steps, the whole tavern listening to the clumping and banging above our heads as the men searched from room to room. I had the feeling they hardly dared come down without at least one slave, so when they finally descended empty-handed, that overseer near boiled himself dry. He suddenly spied the heap of skins Erik had left in the corner of the room. Like a child in a tantrum, he threw one of the pelts across the floor. It landed at my feet, and there, in full view, were the bloodstains from Jacob's lacerated back. I froze, terrified to breathe, never mind respond.

'Ha!' He whirled toward me. 'Na, let me tell you what that is! It is the blood o' ma slave! It is the blood from my property when you stole it!' One by one he lifted the other skins and spread them on the floor. 'All these skins have been scraped clean o' fat an' flesh. Why then, is this skin covered in blood?'

Fury rose within me. Slavery was something I couldn't stomach. I hadn't been born to it and couldn't become accustomed to it. I looked steadily at that pig of a man. *You overfed, sweating pile of fat,* I thought to myself, *you think I'm afeared of you!*

'That blood is not the blood of yer slave!' I snapped. Turning toward the window, I brushed back my hair so my wound was in full view. 'See this?' I seethed. He peered at my swollen cheek with a combination of curiosity and contempt for my suffering. 'I was attacked by a bear! It slashed its claw right through my cheek. My jacket was so drenched in blood the big man had to cut it off and burn it! He wrapped me in that pelt and carried me to safety, and if you're not satisfied, he shot the bear, and the skin is lying there before you as proof!'

My da was right. I was a brazen-faced little imp.

He glared at me with the black, beady eyes of a crow. He knew he was beaten. His men shifted uncomfortably, aware of the humiliation. Spinning on his little hog feet, he headed for the door. A long, quiet breath escaped my lips, but that little fried-in-fat man abruptly stopped and turned back toward me. 'Then tell me this,' he sneered, 'if that man has gone north, why has he left all his skins here?'

He put his hands on his hips and rocked back and forth in triumph. I wasn't prepared for this question. Panic flooded up my spine. The whole plan was about to unravel. I searched for an answer, something he would believe, but couldn't think of one single reason why Erik would leave behind his precious skins. This murderous man was moments from realising Erik hadn't gone north. All the deceiving had been for nothing. We would be dragged before the courts. Even hanged!

'Because we buy all his skins.' The quiet voice belonged to Maggie. 'There is good profit to be made, sir. I sell the skins to passing travellers, or to the townsfolk here, or settlers who come for provisions.'

My heart lurched from despair to joy! The overseer gave me a surly look, then without another word, marched outside, his henchmen following like sheep. As the door closed behind them, the tavern erupted! Discussion and debate on every last detail of the overseer was the order of the day: his character, his fine southern clothes, even his speak. Maggie put her arms around my shoulders and hugged me.

'I'm proud of you, William.' I breathed in her perfume, those pretty, pink marsh roses I used to gather for Ma. 'Now, I must find Erik and tell him it's safe to return. Can I depend on you to serve the customers while I'm gone?'

I would have run myself ragged for those green eyes, and as it happened, I almost did. I ladled broth into bowls, served stew, fetched bread, cut cheese, scraped plates, wiped tables, mopped up spills and carried in firewood. And as though all this was not enough, I also had to serve drinks. This was not my strong point. A thickset man, hairy, breath like retting flax, leaned toward me over the counter and barked, 'Gimme a Mimbo, boy, and be quick about it, my mouth is as dry as a dead bear's arse.'

'A Mimbo, sir?'

'You ain't heard of a Mimbo?' he growled. 'Then gimme a Flip.'

'Um, a Flip, sir?'

I thought he was going to clout me. Fortunately, Maggie returned at that timely moment and poured strong ale into a mug, added an egg, some rum, a little dark molasses and gave it a good shake. She then took the red-hot poker from the fire and plunged it into the mix, which spluttered and frothed and smelled like burnt honey, but that man threw his coins on the table and seemed highly satisfied.

We stayed a further three days at the tavern until Maggie mentioned the owner, George Gibson, would be returning. Apparently, he'd gone to Philadelphia to renew his liquor licence.

'Then it is time to take our leave,' announced Erik. 'We will be on our way in the morning.' I reluctantly agreed because I loved the tavern. There was always so much of interest: farmers, labourers, merchants and traders all discussing the politics of the day. There were noisy card games, and an Irishman with a pocket fiddle played of an evening for those with the legs for jigs and reels!

When the tavern finally emptied, I cleared the dirty plates and mugs, placed them to soak in a half barrel of water in the scullery, then swept the floor and wiped the tables. 'Thank you kindly for your help, William.' Maggie's tender voice almost turned me into a heap of mush at her feet. I could feel my face flame, but all I could mumble in return was a bashful, 'Good night.'

I watched her disappear into the scullery, her auburn curls bobbing around her shoulders, then climbed the stairs to my chamber and peered through the glass. The outside lamp was still burning, and in the glow, I could see snowflakes tumbling like goose feathers. It was going to be sharp as a sword out there tomorrow, and with the arrival of snow, I knew it would soon be time for Erik to bid me farewell.

THE FRENCHMAN

Next morning the world was white as a pigeon egg. I knew the snow had settled even before I pulled the drape because the rolling carts had lost their rumble and the light was different – creamy, like the top of the milk. Wiping the wet window with my sleeve, I gazed along the street. Children were throwing snowballs, while women scolded from doorways about soaking clothes, chills and certain death. All mas are the same.

Maggie wrapped a small block of bone jelly and some stew for our evening meal, then kissed my cheek with her soft, warm lips. I was truly sorry to leave her because she was as kind and beautiful a creature as ever lived.

Leaving Erik to bid her farewell, I carried the skins outside, screwing up my eyes against the bright, cloudless sky. Snow smothered the outhouse roof and the window ledges. It hugged the path, lay lumpy on the firewood and steepled the barn walls with drifts. If James had been with me, we would have jumped and rolled and snowballed in that untouched sheet of perfect white until it looked like curdled milk, but I had a packhorse to load.

Erik finally appeared, flinging on his beaver hat. 'Come, William, we must away! We are heading for the Wauwaset River, or the Brandywine as it is known by the English.' He tightened the girth strap around Thor's belly and seemed content to depart, but Maggie's eyes were brimming with tears. She loved him, I was certain of that. I wondered why he didn't stay, but he must have had his reasons. Perhaps he still loved his wife, even though she'd been dead these long years. Like swans, some folk mate for life.

Pulling up my hood, I lowered my head against the teeth of winter and followed Erik down King Street and into open fields where snowflakes floated around us like apple blossom.

Now, I have always been a champion daydreamer. If left long enough to my own thoughts, I become the rider of the greatest horse at Derry Fair, or a prize-winning wrestler – the only small, bone-skinny fourteen-year-old boy in the whole world to gain victory at collar-and-elbow. In my world of daydreams, I could float away from hunger and all the worries crowding my thoughts, and most times only a slap across the head from Da would wake me from my imaginings.

It was in that quiet forest, I realised I had lost my childish dreams. Since the attack on the settlement, those foolish fantasies had disappeared, never to return. In their place were the hard truths of life – food, shelter and work – and I was so occupied with them, I had quite a jolt when Erik suddenly pulled Thor to a halt. Tugging off his beaver hat, he strained toward a distant sound, then gave a puzzled grin. 'Can you hear singing?'

I listened. Someone was badly out of tune and cracking on the high notes. If that was singing, then I was Ireland's greatest fiddler.

Dismounting, we hid under the trees because singing or not, this was a desolate place. Presently, a man dressed head to toe in furs and riding a grey horse rounded the bend. Erik gave a low chortle of recognition. Stepping from the trees, he called, 'Pierre!'

The man pulled up his horse in surprise. 'Dutch? *Dutch!* Upon my soul! You old rogue!' Sliding down from the saddle, he crunched across the snow toward Erik, arms wide and welcoming. 'Good to see you, my old friend!'

They embraced like two woolly beasts. I could see now he was older than Erik, with flecks of silver in his hair and beard.

'William, come here, boy!' At Erik's beckoning, I crawled from my hiding place. 'William, this is Pierre Bazaillon, an explorer from New France.'

I pulled off a glove and offered my hand. 'Good day to you, sir. I'm right glad to make yer acquaintance.'

'Ah-ha! A leetle Irish cub!' He gave my cold fingers a firm shake as though we'd known each other all our lives. I liked him. He was a jolly sort. His large belly wobbled when he laughed and his brown eyes were open and honest.

'What brings you zis way, Dutch? Is not New York your winter 'ome?'

'It is a long story, my friend! I had hoped to reach the Brandywine, but the journey has been slow, and the light will soon fade. Will you bide with us and share a meal?'

Pierre's ruddy, plump cheeks beamed. 'Zat would indeed be welcome! It 'as been a long day and I would be glad of a fire and company.'

I helped the two men chop saplings and branches, paying attention to the straightness and length of the wood, and with Erik's help, learned how to make a sound shelter. Clearing a small area of snow, we tied the branches together at the top, spread them as wide as possible, threw skins around the frame, then roped them in place. Erik lit a low fire inside, then unrolled the last two skins, and by the time Maggie's rabbit stew was hot, long, black shadows were creeping over the snow.

Sitting snugly around the fire, Pierre turned his attention to me. 'Tell me, young William, 'ow came you into ze company of zis giant?'

'My folk were killed by Natives,' I replied hotly, 'and when I find them, I'll pay them back for what they did!' The words spilt over my lips without hesitation because I had given the matter serious consideration. I was going to find the Natives responsible, then, single-handed, kill them all. That was my plan; the plan of a fourteen-year-old boy. A concerned glance passed between the two men. *You can pity me all you want*, I thought, *but someday I will have my revenge!* Without passing comment on my plan, Pierre nodded toward my injured face. 'Is zat your stitching on ze boy's cheek, Dutch?'

'William was attacked by a bear. I had to close the wound.'

'Ah, you 'ave been brave for one so young.'

Climbing down from my anger, I sheepishly replied, 'Oh, it was nothing.'

Those two men laughed to such an extent I felt my cheeks colour. It was in good sport though, and after we shared the meal, I listened to Pierre as he recounted his life because he could tell a good tale. 'I 'ave often 'ad dealings wiz ze Natives. I speak zer languages and 'ave traded wiz zem for years. I waz also imprisoned for a short while, but zat waz in my younger days.'

'Put in gaol? For what reason?' I asked, fascinated.

'To keep me out of trouble!' he replied with a wink. 'I even 'ad to ransom one of my own brozers from the Iroquois many years ago!' That word again, Iroquois; the mighty Haudenosaunee. 'When did we last meet on zis road, Dutch? Some eight or nine years since? If you remember, zer 'ad been a murder.'

Erik nodded. 'I remember it well.'

I perked up, someone had been killed? 'I beg you, sir, tell me what happened.'

Pipe in hand, Pierre crossed his legs, and settled himself for the story.

'I was searching for a man called John De Burt, a trader from a place called Snaketown. Burt and his friend, Thomas Wright, 'ad been drinking at De Burt's 'ouse at Snaketown wiz Natives from ze Minsi tribe. It is against ze law to sell alcohol to Natives, so De

Burt 'ad already broken zat law. Apparently, an argument occurred between Wright and one of ze Natives, and in fear, De Burt and Wright fled into ze 'ouse and bolted ze door. Ze Natives became very angry and broke into ze 'ouse. Now, you might find zis 'ard to believe, but it is true; De Burt filled 'is 'ands wiz dung from a piss pot and zrew it at ze Natives! Wright fled for 'is life and 'id in the chicken 'ouse, but 'e was found by Natives and killed. It was ze first time Natives killed an Englishman in zat region and it frightened many settlers – zey began to fear for zer lives.'

'Did De Burt escape?'

'Indeed 'e did, and since ze Natives 'ad gone 'unting for ze winter, no punishment could be decided on until ze spring. 'Owever, it was agreed by ze court, zat ze true fault lay wiz De Burt, so a warrant waz issued for 'is arrest. 'E 'ad fled, of course, but I was certain 'e would be punished someday, and not by our courts – and I was right.'

'What do you mean, "not by our courts"?'

'Natives 'ave long memories. Zey would never forget such insulting be'aviour. Five years later in '32, Natives killed John De Burt, 'is wife Mary and seven of zer twelve children. Ze five remaining children fled to kin in Virginia.'

As the night wore on, I lay curled by the smouldering logs and thought of Pierre's astounding story. It was strangely comforting to think those five children must have carried a heart-twisting hatred for Natives, just like me. I wondered if their loathing had lessened over the years, or if it remained as raw as the day their parents had been killed? Had they found a way through their misery, or was it, even now, eating them alive like a gut worm?

Eventually, I slumbered, well used to the sound of Erik's breathing, but Pierre – his snoring rattled the shelter poles. I wouldn't have been surprised to find the vibrations had flattened the entire forest by morning. It was one long night.

When dawn finally streamed through a chink at the bottom of the shelter, I quietly pulled on my boots, pushed back the flap, and duck-e-downed out into the frosty air. The land lay quiet as a newborn lamb. Giant evergreens draped in snow sparkled around me as I tramped through the trees to check the snares Erik had placed the previous night. When I returned with a frozen rabbit, the two men were awake and the fire was ablaze. Erik melted snow in a pot for his chocolate, while Pierre chopped the rabbit with his axe, and before long the welcome smell of cooking meat filled the shelter. Sitting cross-legged in the warmth, I studied those two men. Their ability astounded me. There seemed no circumstance they couldn't survive. Erik had little or no money, but what he did have was sufficient for his needs and he was content. Perhaps that was the secret: contentment. But how was I to find my way to that place of peace? I was stuck in a fathomless pit of guilt and hate that clung to me as though branded on my skin.

When the meal was over we dismantled the shelter. Erik made a rope hammock and slid the poles along Samson's flank, pushing several tightly rolled skins on top. I knew I would be alone that night, but I didn't fret. That good man had delayed his journey long enough and had taught me all I needed to survive. Pierre gave me a hearty slap on the back that near knocked me over, then wished me farewell and good fortune. As he disappeared along the snowy path in the direction of Lancaster, I swung myself up on the saddle and followed Erik through the forest, the trees around me glistening beneath a bright, butterfly-blue sky.

All too soon Brandywine Creek ran before us and we halted by the side of the river where, despite the sunshine, the ground remained as hard as granite. As hard as parting. As hard as leaving. It seemed to me my life was made up of farewells. I would never again see my kin, or Reverend Bertram, or Maggie, or Pierre, and now this big Dutchman.

'This is where I take my leave, William. I must head north, but you can cross the river here. The sun has weakened the ice and Samson can wade to the far bank with ease,' he advised. 'There is still daylight enough for you to reach a river the Natives call the Mohorhoottink. There are cattails all along the water's edge and three pine trees set back from the bank like a three-cornered hat. Set camp between them, it is a safe place to spend the night.'

I struggled for any words that would make light of my sadness, but failed miserably.

'I'm rightly beholden to you, Erik,' I managed, my voice suddenly husky. 'Reckon I would have died without yer help.' I knew I would forever remember him sipping warm chocolate in the early morning mist.

Pulling his leather satchel across his knees, he flipped open the flap. 'Before we part, I have something for you.' He handed me a thin, coiled, plaited string. 'It is a fishing line made from birch bark fibres.'

'I'm very much obliged, Erik! It's exactly what I need!' The line unrolled to about six feet in length; the strands so tightly and neatly intertwined no river fish could ever break it. With a combination of sadness and gratitude, I held out my hand to that good man for the last time. 'I can never repay yer kindness, Erik. You saved my life. I'll never forget you.'

His large palm folded around my fingers. 'Nor I forget you, my young friend. God bless you, boy.'

I wanted to say so much more. I wanted him to know he had restored my spirit, that because of him I could again face the future, but I couldn't find the words. As he turned along the north path, pulling the packhorse behind him, I felt stupidly cold inside, as though a small flame had been blown out by a chill wind. Reaching the bend, he swivelled in the saddle, and raising an arm, gave a last, long wave. I stood in the stirrups calling, 'Farewell Erik! Farewell!' Then he rounded the bend, disappeared from view and from my life.

The Mohorhoottink was just as Erik had described: brown, wilted cattail leaves poking through the snowy bank and three majestic pines, the branches of each touching the others like age-old friends holding hands. With the shelter up and a low fire glowing, an eager feeling of satisfaction swept over me. Instead of cursing the past, I found myself looking toward the future. Instead of dreading the search for work, I was excited by what lay ahead. Only one more day's ride and I would again be in that great town with all its sights and smells! A journey that had seemed all but impossible at the outset, was now almost at an end.

It occurred to me that with my new line I could catch fish, not only for a meal that evening, but to sell in Philadelphia, and so have a little money until I found work. So satisfied was I with myself that I crunched noisily along the bank, fearlessly humming without a care, and leaving my fowler and knife in the shelter.

Upstream, two black-billed Whistling swans paddled silently across the river like large, white balls of cotton on the dark water. The skeleton of an old, dead tree lay on the bank; its bark-stripped, sun-bleached branches stretching like arms toward the sky as though begging for one more day of life. I stamped, hard, on one of the smaller branches. A loud *crack* echoed through the trees – announcing my presence to the whole world. Undaunted, I tied my new line to the branch, fumbled in my pocket for a fish hook, attached a squirming grub, then lowered the line between the creeping ice flows bordering the banks.

Content with my achievements so far, I stood on the snow-covered bank, closed my eyes in the last warm rays of the sun, and waited for a fish to bite. I have since learned it isn't wise to close your eyes when alone in the wilderness because danger is a cunning beast. There was a startled whoosh of wings and a sudden 'woo-hoo' as the swans took hurried flight. My eyes snapped open. A wolf. Twenty yards at most. Its stare locked on mine. Dread crept over my flesh. My heart hammered a desperate warning. I suddenly realised I hadn't a single weapon! My only hope was the river – the ice-cold river! My coat would drown me. Trembling, I grappled with the belt. The buckle clinked on the snow. The wolf began to run! A few more strides and its fangs would sink into my flesh! Tearing my arms from the coat, I whirled toward the river and threw myself into the black, icy water!

Crushing cold shivered me with shock. All around was darkness. My thrashing limbs fought a bubbling battle up toward the light. At last, I broke the surface, choking and gasping for air. I glanced toward the bank. Wolves are good swimmers, but mercifully it hadn't followed me into the water. I had to get to the far bank – out of this killing cold, but the river was widening and the flow quickening. I clawed the surface like a desperate drunkard, but the current was too strong. Roaring water drowned my screams. I crashed over boulders and spun through frothing, white water. Rocks battered my body and grazed my skin. A sudden pain ricocheted up my left arm. I howled. The river tossed me where it wanted – into broken branches and jagged driftwood – until, finally, it spat me into calmer waters, where the current pushed my shivering limbs toward the bank.

My legs were numb. My fingers wouldn't bend. I knew by the odd shape of my left arm it was broken. In desperation, I tore at tree roots with my other hand, trying to haul myself onto the bank, but the searing cold had paralysed every muscle.

All the weeks I had struggled to survive flashed before my eyes. All my efforts to reach Philadelphia had come to nothing. To be defeated at the last because of my own stupidity was almost unbearable. And what of poor Samson? There was no one to untie him. He would die from thirst and hunger or be eaten by wolves. Damn! *Damn!* I wanted to scream in protest at my fate, but the icy water was creeping higher. It washed over my lips. Over my nose.

Struggling to breathe, I tried to cling to the bank, but my fingers wouldn't grip. I was sinking.

The cold twisted my senses, blurring my sight. Blindness crept over me, settling like muslin on my eyes. In that grey, terrifying world, only my sense of smell remained, and it suddenly brought to me the fragrance of yellow meadowsweet, golden gorse and marsh marigold. The scent grew fierce and thick about me. Caring little how such an incredible thing could happen, I strained upward for more of my grandma's perfume, slowly rising until my shoulders breached the water. Again, I tried to haul myself from the freezing flow, but this time, some unseen force below gently pushed me upward. Scrabbling frantically at the roots and vines, I heaved myself at last onto the snowy bank and lay gasping with exhaustion. But the cold had not only invaded my body, it had penetrated my very spirit. It had drained me to the core. There was no fight left in me. I was finished.

Defeated, I slipped into unconsciousness; a deep, deathly sleep that folded its icy fingers around my soul.

MËLËK

I was warm. Wonderfully warm. Long before I opened my eyes, I could feel every toe-tingling part of my body was wrapped in heavenly heat. So this was paradise. *Ouch!* I winced. Any hopes I might be in the presence of the Almighty were suddenly dashed by the pain in my arm and a body that ached as though it had been wrung through a mangle.

Blinking away the blur, I found, to my relief, my sight had returned and I could see my surroundings. I was in some sort of shelter. But how did I get here? Who did it belong to? Too frightened to move, I kept my lashes low and let my eyes roam, furtively, about the place.

It was a small shelter, just large enough for six or eight people. Above me, arched saplings covered with bark formed the frame. Bunches of tobacco leaves and wild mint had been tied to the highest points to dry. My eyes slid sideways. I was lying near a low, smouldering fire. Wisps of grey smoke curled upward to a small gap in the roof, while around the walls sat several hunting bows, clay pots, rolled furs, a quiver of arrows, corn cobs, wooden bowls and a basket of white bone beads. I glanced down. A thick, warm bearskin covered my wounded body and I could see my clothes folded neatly near the fire.

A small movement caught my eye. An elderly, grey-haired woman, her skin brown as a walnut, was sitting cross-legged near the doorway of the shelter. She wore a leather tunic with small shells stitched around the neckline and hem, and was quietly humming to herself as she plaited thin strips of bark.

Alarm scythed through my senses. This woman was a Native! I was in a Native shelter! Sweat began to ooze from my skin. My chest tightened and I had a sudden desire to run for my life!

She hadn't noticed I was awake. Should I reach for my clothes and make a dash for it? I wasn't certain I could stand, never mind run. And how was I supposed to escape with a broken arm? My head throbbed. Slowly, I slipped my right hand from under the cover, and reached toward the pain. A sticky paste had been mashed into a gash on my forehead. My fingertips searched my cheek. Mercifully, the stitches had held. Trying not to draw attention to myself, I carefully lifted the edge of the cover and peeped beneath the fur. Someone had straightened and splinted my arm.

This final movement was noticed. The woman looked up from her work and without a word, draped a short fur cape around her shoulders, scrambled to her feet, pushed back the hide door flap and stepped outside. I heard an exchange of words, which didn't help my fear. What were they planning? A moment later, a tall boy, hair black as charcoal, entered the shelter. I tensed. He seemed about my age, but taller, broader and better fed – his ribs weren't poking out as mine were.

He wore only a few simple garments: a length of leather from his waist to his knees, leather leggings and boots, and a small squirrel pouch on a thong around his neck. In his hand he carried a skin mantle, which he laid on the ground, then, without shifting his dark-eyed gaze from me, sat cross-legged in silence at my feet. It was the penetrating look of a hunter at the hunted. I hardly dared breathe. Pulling the cover to my chin I stared back at him, and there we stayed, studying one another for quite some time, neither of us speaking because there seemed little point; I couldn't understand Native words and assumed he wouldn't understand my speak. He didn't look as though he was about to torture me, but it's hard to tell about such things. Had I escaped the river to be slaughtered here?

'What is your name?' the hunter asked, breaking the silence. His words gave me a jolt. He had spoken in English. Despite his strong native accent, I understood him perfectly.

'William – my name is William,' I stammered.

'I am Mëlëk. This is my home: my *wikëwam*. You are surprised I speak your tongue, but I learn from trader, hunter, settler and trapper. I also journey many time to Philadelphia with my father. All people in that town speak English,' he replied as though reading my thoughts.

This was bewildering and not what I had expected. 'How long have I been here?'

'We found you by the river yesterday. You were cold. We put you in the *pimëwakàn*. It is a place of hot stone. My father straighten your arm,' he explained.

I expected savagery from Natives, yet these people had not only saved me from certain death on the river bank, but tended my wounds. Now, I had been brought up to mind my manners. If Ma had been there she would have wagged the finger at me.

'In yer speak, what is the word for "thank you"?' I ventured.

He allowed a slight curl of his lips. '*Wanishi, wan-ish-i.*'

'Then, *wan-ish-i*, Mëlëk, for saving my life.'

To my surprise, his hard stare softened a little, so I took courage. 'What is the name of yer tribe?' hoping he wouldn't say the dreaded Haudenosaunee.

'We are the Lenni Lenape. In winter we spend many week in the forest hunting. We were returning when we found your garment in the snow.'

The snow. The shelter. Samson! I threw back the cover.
My garments lay within reach, Da's belt curled neatly on top.
I stretched for my linen drawers. 'Mëlëk, I thank you for yer
kindness. I am indeed grateful to you, but I must return to the
river for my horse. There are wolves. I left him tethered. He is in
great danger.'

'Your horse is in our camp. He is safe.'

I halted. 'My horse is here?'

'We found your track and followed it to your shelter. You built
it well.' Now he was complimenting my building skills. This was
truly puzzling. 'We also saw the mark of the wolf.'

'I-I jumped in the water. It was my only way of escape.'

'It was a wise thing to do.'

I began pulling my drawers over my feet, wriggling them up
over my hips, struggling to tie the waist string with one hand and
my teeth. Who would have thought the use of only one arm would
make everything so difficult! He didn't offer to help me.

'You are small as an unlicked cub, or a *namètët* – little fish.' He
said this as though he was the first person ever to bring it to my
attention. 'How old are you?'

'I'm fourteen.'

His brown eyes circled with white. '*Fourteen?*' he exclaimed in
disbelief. I wanted to fling something at him. It wasn't my fault I was
small. I ate every scrap of food I could find!

'Why are you alone?'

Panic gripped me. I didn't want him to know my kin had been
murdered by people just like him, so avoided the question.

'I was on my way to Philadelphia when the wolf attacked. I got
no wish to remain in this land. I hope to find a ship and return to
my own country.'

He frowned as if he had misunderstood. 'You do not wish to
remain here?' I shook my head, no. But still, he was not satisfied.
'You do not wish to settle in this land when you are a man?'

'I desire nothing more than to return across the ocean to my home. I have a longing for my own people.'

I couldn't tell why, but this piece of information seemed to lower a wall between us because he suddenly asked, 'Are you hungry?'

Now, as far back as I can remember, no one had ever asked me that question because it was obvious to most that I was half-starved, but I replied politely, 'I would gladly take some nourishment, Mëlëk. Thank you kindly.'

'Here is your clothing,' he offered, laying the dry garments at my side. 'Leave the paste on your head. It will halt the green poison.'

I reckon he meant pus.

Climbing into my garments with one hand proved difficult. I managed to wriggle into my shirt, leaving the left sleeve hanging empty, but trying to get into my breeches, I toppled and crashed down on the bowl of beads. They soared into the air, hit the roof, then hailed down on us like musket shot.

Lying in a heap on the ground didn't help my broken arm or battered body, but worse, I could feel my face colouring with embarrassment. As I scrambled around trying to retrieve the beads and apologise for my bungling, Mëlëk's face crinkled into a smile. His cheeks were bursting. How dare he laugh at me! Grabbing a handful of beads, I threw them at him! He swung a shoulder toward me in defence, then snatching up the beads, returned fire!

They bounced around the roof and walls as we dipped and dived. Grabbing the corn husks from the floor, I hurled them at him. He flung them back at me. Next, the wooden plates went spinning from wall to wall like sycamore seeds. It was a miracle we didn't set fire to the place!

Suddenly the door flap lifted and a brown scalp ducked into the *wikëwam*. Now, a boy is one thing, but standing before me was a tall, muscular, tattooed Native. Breathless, we ceased our caper immediately. The blood rushed from my head, no doubt trying to hide in some other part of my body. I wished I could hide with it. Corn, string, plates, furs, beads and bowls littered the mats. Our hijinks had also brought down some of the tobacco leaves from the roof. I readied myself for a good scolding, or worse. Da would have skelped my rump.

The man folded his arms, raised his brow and gave Mëlëk a quizzical look. Mëlëk mumbled something, but instead of a slap across the head, the man pointed to the floor and even I could understand he was telling Mëlëk to arrange things in their proper order. As he turned to leave, I whispered quickly, 'Mëlëk, is this man yer father?'

He nodded. 'This is my father, Òpalanie. He say it is time to eat.'

'Sir!' I ventured. Halting by the door flap, he turned to face me. 'I thank you for saving me and splinting my arm. I would have died had you not found me. *Wan-ish-i.*'

I spoke slowly as Mëlëk translated, and had the impression his da was surprised. Perhaps he hadn't expected thanks from the little white settler boy.

Alone again, we gazed at the confusion around our feet. Mëlëk picked up one small bone bead and tossed it toward me, grinning. It was a mock throw; something between friends. I smiled, but didn't throw it back.

When everything was neatly arranged, I wriggled into the rest of my clothes. What a sight I must have been; my body bruised and scratched, green paste in my hair and staining my shirt, a broken arm and stitches the length of my face. I was relieved when Mëlëk brought my coat because I couldn't bear to lose it. Slipping it around my shoulders, I pulled on my boots and followed him outside into another world.

For the first time in my life, I was gazing at a Native village. More than thirty *wikëwams* circled a large, long, bark-covered building. At various places around the edge of the camp, deer and beaver carcasses hung from wooden cross-poles, while neat rows of duck and turkey lay in the snow, ready for plucking. Old, dry branches and chopped wood lay in tangled piles, ready to feed the many fires, yet the camp was quiet. There were few people out in the cold. I spied several men warmly dressed in skins and armed with hatchets and bows and took them to be sentries on watch. My guts fluttered at the sight of their weapons; it was the first time I'd seen armed Natives since the attack. Silently, they studied me as though I was a young buck to be hunted.

Mëlëk beckoned me across the well-trodden snow, but as we entered the longhouse, fear halted my steps. This was where everyone had gathered. A hundred faces turned and stared at me. All chatter ceased. I had only one thought – *I must escape before it's too late!* Mëlëk, seeing my fright, clutched my good arm and pulled me around the wall to a low platform, where I sat close to him, feeling more than a little nervous.

Two large fires blazed, the smoke twisting like vines up through holes in the centre of the roof. The smell of cooking was mouth-watering; corn and beans simmered in clay pots and juicy meat sizzled on hot stones. There was flatbread and bean stew, deer, turkey and rabbit meat, smoked fish, pumpkins, corn patties, walnuts, hickory nuts and chestnuts, mushrooms, cooked cattail roots, dried cranberries and plums. I'd never seen such a feast. We wouldn't have eaten this amount in a six month! I turned to Mëlëk. 'Do you always have this much food?'

He shook his head. 'No, tonight is a celebration, then we do not eat for two week.'

I stared at him, panic-stricken. 'No food for two weeks!'

He didn't look at me, but a dribble of juice escaped his lips as his cheeks dimpled, and I realised he was trying not to laugh.

'Mutton head!' I said under my breath, with a grin.

The longhouse was divided in two; the trappings of family life in one part and everyone else crowded into the remaining space. Four huge posts, each with a carved face, stood like guardians at the four corners of the building. Older boys were playing with what looked like dice, while the younger children, squealing with delight, chased each other around the room. It reminded me of James and the days when we ran through the fields like spring foals let out of the barn for the first time. But that memory belonged to another world, another time.

The meal began and Mëlëk gave me so much food it overflowed from the bowl and dripped onto my breeches. I ate with great satisfaction, happy to have a full stomach, then sat quietly listening to all their talk and trying not to do anything foolish or draw attention to myself. When the meal was finished, the dancing began, and they were just like the Irish! Nothing settles a meal like a good foot-stomping jig! The women followed the men to the rhythm of bone whistles, turtle shells and hide-covered drums; singing, swaying and spinning. The music was so lively I don't know how the roof stayed on that building.

I didn't dance. I didn't know the steps, and even if Mëlëk had tried to teach me, I would probably have fallen over my own feet. In truth, I was still a mite weary. My arm was paining me so badly I could have happily laid myself down and slept, but Mëlëk suddenly reappeared, red-faced, shiny and breathless from dancing, and beckoned me to follow him. Lifting my coat, I edged around the walls toward the doorway.

Outside was cool and quiet after the heat of the longhouse. The wind had dropped and a blanket of stars twinkled above the evergreens. The warriors paced around, attentive to any strange sound or movement. One particular warrior drew my attention. There was a certain nobility about him. A head taller than any other man, he carried himself like a king, yet his black gun-hole eyes made every nerve in my body shudder with fear. To my horror, he left his post and followed us across the snow to Mëlëk's *wikëwam*. Every few steps I couldn't help but glance behind, wondering if I was going to feel a knife in my back.

Inside the *wikëwam*, two men and a woman were sitting around the fire in a fog of baccy fumes. They beckoned me to sit with them; Mëlëk at my side. A thin-faced man with a tattooed brow, an animal pouch around his neck and a skin mantle draped over one shoulder, was introduced as Chief Lapowinsa. I recognised Òpalanie, and Mëlëk presented his mother, Nipën. I liked her immediately because she smiled and seemed a motherly sort. The warrior who had followed us sat beside Òpalanie, and I soon learned he was a war-chief named Kuwèmu. I tried to avoid his solemn gaze, rolling the name Koo-wem-oo silently around my tongue. It was a name I would never forget.

When everyone was settled, Chief Lapowinsa spoke and Mëlëk translated, 'They ask how old you are, William. I cannot answer for you.'

'I'm fourteen,' I sighed, watching their glances of dismay.

'Why were you alone in the forest?' There would be no avoiding the question this time because they were all sitting quietly and attentively, eagerly awaiting my reply. What would they think? I took a deep breath. 'My kin are dead. My ma and da, and my sister and brothers were – they were – killed by Natives,' I mumbled. To my surprise, their expressions remained unchanged, yet I felt certain I'd crossed some unmarked line and shifted uncomfortably, studying the glowing embers to avoid their eyes.

'How long since you left the land of King George?' asked Mëlëk.

'I didn't live in the land of King George. I lived in a country called Ireland,' I corrected. Mëlëk looked surprised. Brows were raised and more questions followed.

'If you are not from the country of King George, why do you speak the English word?' he continued.

'England conquered Ireland, so we speak English,' I answered truthfully. I knew little of the history of Limavady but continued with what I could remember, 'I lived in Ulster in the town of Limavady. My ancestors came from Scotland over one hundred years ago...'

They stared blankly at me. Even Mëlëk looked baffled. There was no point in offering further explanation – the history of Ulster is confusing enough for the people who live there. I began again in simpler terms, 'I came here with my family hoping for a better life. It was a long journey – more than seventy days at sea. We were fortunate to survive. Many died of sickness or thirst, and still more during a mighty storm.'

I was unsure if Mëlëk understood every word, but I believe he got the sense of it because they seemed vastly interested. Finally, Chief Lapowinsa bid me tell them how I'd injured my face.

'I was attacked by a bear, sir. Fortunately, a Dutchman shot the animal, but it fell on me and broke my ribs. Then I suffered a fever. But for the grace of that Dutchman, I would have died. He stitched my face and tended me until I recovered.'

There was a general murmuring. Mëlëk whispered, 'They are amazed at your journey and your many injury, yet still you live!'

The door flap was suddenly flung open and three boys and a young girl, glowing from the dancing, burst in and wriggled down by the fire. Chief Lapowinsa and Kuwèmu took the opportunity to leave, beckoning Òpalanie to follow them. Mëlëk grabbed the two youngest boys as I used to hold James – my arm around his neck until he squealed.

'These are my brother,' he grinned. 'Sënihële is six year. This little cub, Kёntke, is four year, and *that* boy,' he pointed to a sultry figure hunkered by the fire, 'is my brother Tiyas. He is almost a man and at war with the world.' Tiyas barely acknowledged me. 'This is my sister Òxehёmu,' Mëlëk continued, 'she is ten year.' He swung her up in his arms, where she giggled and wriggled, and for the briefest of moments, sounded just like Lizzy.

Under warm covers of thick fur, we lay sprawled around the fire. I stared at the roof in the flickering firelight, watery sorrow creeping over my lashes. The evening had been much more than I could ever have imagined. I didn't want to sleep because I knew when I awoke it would be daylight, and I would have to take my leave. I'd been terrified of these people, yet they had welcomed me and provided me with nourishment. Tomorrow I would be alone again – with a broken arm. I couldn't even load the fowler if I was attacked by robbers on the road and I certainly wouldn't be offered work in Philadelphia. I suddenly realised I was jealous of Mëlëk's life in this happy place. What a raising he must have had, here, where there was food in plenty. Even if he lost his da and ma and all the young'uns spread around the *wikëwam*, the tribe would watch over him. He would never know the depth of loneliness that I endured.

Òpalanie returned and prodded Mëlëk awake. I lay quietly as they spoke in hushed voices, then Mëlëk rolled toward me, his thick hair falling like burnt, black straw around his brown face.

'William, Chief Lapowinsa has sent word. He believe the Great Spirit has protected you many time from death, so must want you to live. You can stay with us until you are well and strong.'

Stunned by this news, I forgot to breathe. I forgot to blink. I forgot everything except Mëlëk's words. Then in a rush of breath, I choked, trying to hide the joy glistening in my eyes. The relief of a condemned man spared the gibbet couldn't have been greater than mine at that moment! The dread of riding alone through dangerous forests vanished, and when I finally found my voice, the words tumbled from my lips like wild horses to be harnessed before they bolted, 'I thank Chief Lapowinsa. Please tell yer folks I'm grateful for their kindness. They needn't fret about feeding me – I know how to hunt.'

He gave a wry smile. 'If you eat as you did in the longhouse, we will all starve.' He pulled the fur cover up around his neck. 'You are brave. You have survived many danger. I will give you a new name. I will call you Aihàmtët.'

'Ai-hàm-tët?' I queried.

'It is our word for a young eagle. An eagle fly alone. It is fearless. It will not run before a storm like other bird. It fly above the cloud. You have risen above the storm. You are a young eagle.'

Mëlëk thought I was fearless. He didn't realise what a coward I truly believed myself to be. I thanked him, and secretly hoped I could live up to this new name.

Òpalanie placed a few wet logs on the fire to smoulder the night away, then he and Nipën settled down to sleep. I watched each small, swirling puff of smoke chase toward the roof. Beyond the walls of the *wikëwam*, I could hear the laughter of stragglers from the longhouse heading back to warm fires. Beside me, Tiyas and Sënihële lay softly snoring, while Òxehëmu slept like Lizzy, quietly. In the firelight, all I could see of Mëlëk was a shovel of black hair poking from under the fur cover. I had made a friend, a Native friend. Tomorrow was going to be the beginning of a very different life.

SMALLPOX

There was nothing I liked better than a gusty day, although I loved the wind no matter how it blew; the gentle breeze of a summer's day, or the flutter that blows the straw in circles, or fierce winter blasts that made me curl my coat against the cold. Yet, I loved it most when it blew from the east because that meant it had come from Ireland. Sucking up cinders from warm Irish chimneys, it raced across the wide ocean as though searching for me. I would set my feet apart, stretch my arms wide, and breathe in the rush until it hit the pit of my lungs, certain I could smell the trace of burning turf from a thousand Irish hearths.

That windy winter passed so quickly I couldn't rightly mind where it had gone, for there had been so much to occupy my time. My broken arm mended, and the more I used the muscles, the stronger they grew. Nipën carefully removed the stitches from my face, which eased the skin as they had been pulling a mite, and gradually all my cuts and bruises healed and I set to work hunting with Mëlëk, eager to bring food to the table.

The Lenape had few horses, so we walked many a mile snaring fox, rabbit and muskrats. We also hunted beaver, duck and turkey, and after the thaw, collected what Mëlëk called *sëpi shukël* from the sugar maple trees; a watery sap to sweeten all manner of foods.

I had thought myself quite a good hunter until I met Mëlëk. He brought down an old buck with a single arrow and was praised by Kuwèmu for his skill. Even in snow, he could creep around the forest with barely a sound, while I seemed heavy-footed and clumsy. When we were a long way from camp, he left markers to find our way home, although nothing a stranger would notice: stones perched at an angle, or three criss-crossed twigs, or a broken branch pointing in the right direction. He was like the North Star. All I had to do was follow.

We talked of many things, he even spoke of spirits as though it was the most natural thing in the world. To my amazement, he explained he had experienced a *linkwehëleokàn* – a spirit vision. I told him of Grandma's mystic presence in my life, something I would not have told another living soul, yet this information seemed only to tighten the bond between us.

On winter evenings, he helped me fashion a hunting bow, I whittled with my knife until that hickory was smooth as an old river pebble and my fingers were nicked and bleeding like Grandma's chin. The wood then had to be heated, but first Mëlëk handed me a small bowl of duck fat and explained the fat would protect the wood from burning. I lathered a good helping of grease along the smooth surface then held the bow over the fire, slowly bending it as the earthy, sweet smell of warm hickory saturated the *wikëwam*. When it was finished, I twanged the taut sinew and felt the vibration sing in my ears. Mëlëk nodded approvingly. It was a good bow.

I also made a quiver from fox skin and became skilled at crafting arrows. When the snow was falling thick, and we were sealed inside by cold that could have cracked a cobblestone, I worked reeds and slender willow branches until I could balance the arrow on one finger, adding or changing feathers at the tail end as needed. It was satisfying work and made me feel useful, and gradually I settled and began to learn a few Lenape words combined with a fair amount of hand-waving.

While the chiefs occupied themselves with the demands of the Council at Philadelphia and problems of land, I realised there was one person who was the true guardian of that tribe: the war-chief, Kuwèmu. I had never known such a man. Shrewd, brave and a master wrestler, he held the soul of those people in his hand. His arms and broad chest were covered in tattoos telling the story of his battles, while across his shoulder blades stretched symbols of the three Lenape clans: wolf, turtle and turkey. If I had been his enemy, I think I would have offered to slay myself, just to save time.

Tall and fierce, he was aware of everything; from strangers on Lenape land to the newest baby born in the camp. Simply standing near him was like being anchored to a painted boulder, which made it all the more startling when one day, he fell from his horse.

It was the day he returned from Philadelphia. He had been attending discussions with the Council over Lenape land. As war-chief, it was not Kuwèmu's position to deal with such affairs, it was more usual for him to go as protector to an Elder or Chief, but this time he had gone alone. He always sat proud and upright on his horse, but that day he suddenly slumped over the horse's neck, then slithered to the hard earth in a tangle of limbs.

Bewildered gasps echoed through the tribe. They had never witnessed any weakness in their beloved war-chief. Moon-eyed panic sent them rushing toward the writhing man, but I grabbed Mëlëk's arm and held him fast. From where I stood, I could see flat, red spots on Kuwèmu's upper arms. Erik's warning sounded in my ears: smallpox! Kuwèmu had been in Philadelphia for ten days, a town where every week there was another outbreak of that hideous disease. If this was smallpox, the entire tribe could perish! I had to get their attention. Waving my arms in the air, I screeched, 'Keep away! *Away!* White man's disease! *Smallpox!*'

The force of my cry squeezed under every *wikëwam* and into every ear, but no one understood my speak, except Mëlëk. His frightened stare locked on mine. '*Smallpox?*'

'He must not be touched!' I pleaded urgently.

Trance-like, he held my gaze only a moment longer, then turned and ran toward the tribe, frantically yelling, '*Tëspehëleokàn! Tëspehëleokàn!*'

Suddenly surprised into action, they scattered like dandelion seeds in the wind.

A mist of beaded sweat clung to Kuwèmu's skin. He searched for every breath; his open mouth begging the breeze to dive down to his lungs. Mèmèkas, his wife, arrived flushed with fright, cries of horror trailing unfinished from her lips. She tried to reach her husband, but firm arms held her back until she finally sank helplessly to the ground, moaning like a winter wind.

'Aihàmtët, what must we do?' Mëlëk pleaded, his lips tightening into a straight, thin line of suppressed fear.

'He must *not* be touched,' I repeated. 'Somehow, he must be taken from this place – from all these people.' I knew what to do, but not how to do it.

To my relief, Òpalanie arrived. Visibly shaken to see his friend in such a state, he knelt beside him and asked, 'Kuwèmu, can you crawl onto a mat?'

Kuwèmu's reply was a feeble nod of the head; he had no energy to speak. Òpalanie ordered two ropes tied to the edges of a deerskin. The stricken war-chief then stretched out an arm, dug his fingernails into the earth and began to drag his infected body onto the large skin. Every movement made him grimace with exertion and pain. It was harrowing to watch. I never thought to see the great man so staggered. The deerskin was then slowly pulled into his *wikëwam*, where Mèmèkas had hurriedly placed a rolled beaver pelt for his head, some skins to cover his body, a wooden cup, plate and spoon, and a bowl of water. Leaving the deerskin and ropes behind, the men withdrew as Kuwèmu pulled a cover over his shivering body, and slipped into battle – a fight he would have to face alone.

A long, high wail suddenly echoed around the camp. Silhouetted against the grey light, an elderly man, draped in the skin of a large mountain lion, swayed toward us like a demon from the underworld. But this was no fiend. It was Pèthakhuwe the medicine man; healer, prophet and keeper of traditions. He was a chilling sight. Deer hooves and animal bones dangled from the claws of the skin, and bird skulls swung from the open jaw on his head. Until that day I'd seen Pèthakhuwe only once; the morning he announced the shad had returned to the river to spawn. This had caused great excitement, and every man who could carry a bow or net had headed toward the river.

He was highly respected. His knowledge of the spirit world had been gathered during a lifetime of learning. I secretly hoped to have no dealings with him because I was afeared he might see me as a young snipper-snapper trying to muddle my way in where I didn't belong. The tribe parted before him like grinning lips, and as he passed, I caught the fresh scent of pine and mint and noticed his fingers were stained green from years of pounding plants. Striding to the door of the *wikëwam*, he gazed silently at Kuwèmu. I shifted nervously, certain he knew nothing of smallpox. If he laid one fingernail on Kuwèmu's shivering body, he might kill us all. Suddenly, he turned toward me, the weight of his gaze shrivelling my confidence. I withered like a cut flower, my head drooping until I could see only my boots. He was surely going to beat the tar out of me for daring to give instruction regarding Kuwèmu. However, when at last he spoke, his voice was surprisingly level and calm, though directed at Mëlëk, not at me.

'Tell me what the white boy knows of *tëspehëleokàn*.'

Nervously, I raised my eyes and spoke with respect, 'Sir, there is no cure for this sickness. There is only one thing we can do: prevent it from spreading. Smallpox can jump like a frog. That's why we mustn't go into the *wikëwam*.'

His gaze was unflinching. 'How long will the sickness last?'

'If it *is* smallpox, blisters will soon appear. He must not be touched until they have healed, which may take many days. Of course, he… he may die before then,' I added quietly.

Pèthakhuwe listened attentively as I used to listen to Reverend Bertram, and I realised what he desired was knowledge. He wanted to understand. He didn't hold himself or his pride above his tribe. He knew he couldn't heal smallpox. The only way he could help was to learn. He was indeed a wise man. Shaking his head, he sighed bitterly and turned to leave.

Now, something was nagging me. A piece of information I had folded and put neatly away on a shelf in my brain. Something I thought would never again be needed.

'Wait!' He half-turned back toward me. 'Sir, I have heard there are Natives in New Scotland who can cure smallpox with a plant!' I cried excitedly.

Mëlëk's quick translation brought an immediate question, 'Which plant?'

I dragged Erik's dusty words from the shelf, 'I can't tell you the name, but I know it has one red flower – and the leaves collect water like a pitcher – then the plant eats the flies that fall into the water!'

Pèthakhuwe spun toward Òpalanie and pointed to the wetlands. A hurried discussion followed. Others joined the debate, some pointing north, some west. An ocean of hope surged through the tribe. With all haste, men headed toward the marshland, spreading like ivy through the trees in search of the precious plant. Mëlëk went with them, briefly explaining before he departed that if the plant was found, they must first appease the plant spirit before carefully uprooting it. That would take time, but was their custom. I was to keep watch over Kuwèmu, as though my knowledge of smallpox gave me magical powers. What was I supposed to do if he took a turn for the worse?

As the hours passed, I sat outside the *wikëwam* with a distraught Mèmèkas, watching Kuwèmu struggling to breathe until, as night descended, the men returned, rippling with excitement, and carrying bright green clumps of veined, tube-shaped leaves topped with a single-stemmed red flower.

For two days, Kuwèmu vomited. Pèthakhuwe tied a small wooden bowl to a long, straight branch and from the doorway, slowly dropped the plant mixture into Kuwèmu's dry mouth. Òpalanie pushed bowls of water inside to entice Kuwèmu to drink, even adding *sëpi shukël* to ease his throat, until finally, drained and pale, the war-chief stopped retching. Mèmèkas believed the mighty man would mend, but from everything Erik had told me, I suspected the worst was galloping toward us, wild as a windstorm.

Mëlëk and I passed by the *wikëwam* early every morning before we went hunting, but the sight of the war-chief four days later, made my skin tingle with horror. His features had all but disappeared under weeping, pus-filled blisters. The lesions would soon cover his entire body. They would fill his mouth and cover his throat, his arms, chest and legs, until not one scrap of untouched flesh remained, then he would choke to death.

Mèmèkas, her eyes red and swollen, sat tortured with despair by the doorway. I felt as useless as a broken button. The plant medicine wasn't working. How foolish I had been to give them hope. As with so many times in my life, I should have kept my gob firmly shut.

Despite the worry of smallpox, there was still work to be done; cutting wood for the fires and hunting deer, or *ayape* as Mëlëk called them. By now, I realised it was Mëlëk's habit never to stick to a path, any path, and he dragged me through bushy undergrowth to where the river current slowed. There we fished for *wisamèkok*, hauling up enough of those whiskered, leather-skinned catfish to last for days.

One day we found a patch of early berries, and were sitting under a large oak tree gorging on their pale green flesh when Mëlëk suddenly set a finger to his lips – a warning. I froze, marvelling how he sensed danger. I had heard nothing, not so much as the snap of a twig, whereas he had already lifted his bow and was halfway up the tree.

Hidden by thick clusters of spring leaves, we perched ourselves on the broad branches and surveyed both sides of the river bank. Movement in the undergrowth thirty yards to our left signalled the enemy.

'Susquehannock,' Mëlëk whispered. 'Two young native on a quest for first blood. They will take whoever they can, especially a child.'

He had told me about the Susquehannock. Many years ago they were almost wiped out by smallpox, but a small number still lived at a place called Kanastoge. They were bitter enemies of the Lenape. Silently, we watched them creep between the trees, drawing ever nearer to the Lenape settlement. In alarm, I pointed to our arrows – could we not scare them away? But Mëlëk simply smirked, 'I do not want them to flee. They must suffer for this. I will warn of their approach.'

He notched an arrow then let it fly high above the trees toward camp. It would be recognised by its feathers as belonging to Mëlëk and need investigation. I was afeared the Susquehannock might hear the *whoosh* as it flew, but without so much as a glance toward them, Mëlëk whispered, 'They hear nothing. They are asshead.'

His English was improving daily.

We waited. The Susquehannock crept ever nearer to the edge of the camp. I marvelled at Mëlëk's calmness because I could barely breathe. Suddenly, I spied five scalp locks creeping toward us through the trees: the warriors! It took little time to capture those Susquehannock. They fought bravely, but two against so many saw them led into camp with their hands bound and women spitting in their faces. They were terrified, it was well marked in their nervous, wide-eyed glances, and they had reason to be because their punishment began immediately.

Now, my guts have a mind to heave when I see torture. I wasn't raised to enjoy the spectacle, although I'd come to understand it was the Native way. Those young men were tied to a pole and held a few feet above the ground, then the Lenape brought flaming torches and began to burn their feet. The sickly, heavy smell of charred meat seeped into the air and clung to my nose. One of the young men showed great bravery. He made no sound except short, sharp grunts as he squirmed; sweat running over the swollen veins on his scarlet face. His companion wasn't so courageous. He howled like a tortured dog. His screams were sickening. Unable to bear it any longer, I edged toward the outer ring of spectators, but still, I could hear his cries. Such a sound, once heard, can never be forgotten. I knew I'd be hearing it in my sleep.

One of the Elders suddenly raised his hand and called, 'Chitkwësikw!' Silence crept through the tribe. Burning torches were lowered, women stopped jeering and children laid their scorched poking-sticks on the ground. I understood very little of the following speak, but I did hear the word tëspehëleokàn – smallpox.

They hauled those two young men onto their burnt feet and dragged them through the camp to Kuwèmu's wikëwam. I expected to hear him choking and see his body a mass of sores, but to my surprise, the blisters hadn't increased. Pustules still covered his skin, but no more than the previous day. Was the plant medicine working?

The two young men were thrust in beside him, and the pole lowered until they had no choice but to kneel by his body, their legs and arms touching his weeping sores. There they remained until dusk, kneeling like a sacrifice and begging for their lives. When darkness began to close in, they were finally hauled a great distance into the forest and thrown a knife so they could free themselves. They would carry that invisible death back to their tribe and it would infect all who touched them.

Now, I thought about what the Lenape had done and decided there was only one thing to say; the New World is a wild and savage place and Natives do what they must to survive. Mëlëk explained tribes are often at war not only with each other, but with settlers, the French and the British. The only certainty was danger and plenty of it.

Three days later, Kuwèmu, the great war-chief of the Lenape, opened his eyes. This was surely a witness to the strength of the man and to the medicine Pèthakhuwe had prepared. His survival was greeted with great relief, especially by me; the medicine had worked, and I felt acquitted by judge and jury. A relieved and smiling Mèmèkas sat by the door with Òpalanie, who told his friend of the Susquehannock Natives and how, single-handed, Kuwèmu had probably destroyed the entire Susquehannock tribe and slept through the whole affair.

The following day, Mëlëk and I were preparing for an afternoon of fishing when to my surprise, Pèthakhuwe came to find us. From beneath his mantle, he drew a small, carved willow stick and placed it in my hand. 'This is for you Aihàmtët, so you will not forget us.'

'It is a prayer stick!' The delight in Mëlëk's eyes told me I was honoured to be given such a gift. In length, the stick was about the span of a man's hand and had three, young eagle feathers attached to one end. I ran my fingers along the wood, caressing the curved lines and breathing in the lingering smell of Pèthakhuwe's hands: cedar, tobacco, bloodroot and the scent of a hundred other plants. I didn't have the words to tell him I would never forget my time in this place and curled my fingers around the wood to keep it safe because it was, and always would be, one of the most precious objects in the world to me.

The day came at last when Kuwèmu's blisters were completely healed. With Mèmèkas by his side, he walked to the new *wikëwam* built for him by a grateful and mightily relieved tribe. Kuwèmu was not a man to show any weakness, but I reckon he barely accomplished that short journey before his knees buckled.

I had explained to Pèthakhuwe that Kuwèmu's old *wikëwam* must be burned, so when dusk had settled, an arrow dipped in warm pine sap was set alight and fired into the bark-covered walls of his old home. Hungry flames stretched for the darkening sky as the demon disease crackled and writhed. In the glow, I could see Kuwèmu watching the flames engulf what could have been his deathbed. I had seen that expression before, but not in the camp of the Lenape. It had marked the face of every survivor aboard ship after the storm. It was the look of an animal that had escaped the trap.

REVENGE

That summer near fried me to a fritter. The grass browned and crunched under our feet as the camp shimmered in the heat. Beanstalks grew higher every day, and as the weeks passed, pumpkins showed the first orange tinges of ripening. Out in the fields, I scythed corn until my shoulders ached and my skin freckled in the sun. It didn't go unnoticed that I was the only male among hordes of women because Lenape men don't occupy themselves with cutting corn, they have other work, so the women had some sport at my expense. They placed corn stalks on my head and a leather skirt around my waist. It was all in jest and I took it as such, parading like a girl through the bright, golden field to shrieks of laughter. I believe the Lenape took a liking to me that day, or at the very least, no longer regarded me with suspicion. I simply became the daft white boy, which was very satisfying and safe.

Mëlëk sat plucking out his body hair. It looked painful to me. I had no intention of ripping out my thick, long locks or pulling out leg hair simply to look handsome for the ladies, not even for the most beautiful girl in camp: Silpel. Her name in English meant Silver, and her dark, smouldering eyes were very inviting, but it was clear from the beginning that no Lenape girl wanted a white boy as a husband. In many ways, I was glad of it. I wouldn't be driven off course; Ireland was my home and where I longed to be.

I realised I must now be fifteen because the day of my birth was in hard winter, and that had long since passed. For the first time in my life, I had enough to eat, and I believe that's what caused me to sprout. I was no longer a skinny little runt. My ribs disappeared under plump flesh and astonishingly, I caught up in height with Mëlëk. I was taller than Da had ever been, or any of my kin in Ireland. If they could see me now!

There was just one problem: my clothes were too small. The sleeves of my shirt were now part way up my arms and the linen fit to burst around my chest. I couldn't button my breeches; only Da's belt prevented them from falling around my ankles. I'd also given up trying to squash my toes in my boots because they nipped and gave me blisters the size of duck eggs, so Mëlëk gave me a pair of his moccasins.

Nipën noticed my tight clothes. Fetching some leather, she carefully cut a long, rectangle piece about a foot in width and five feet in length, then handed it to me with the word, *sàkutakàn* – breechcloth. She had measured well. When the leather was tucked between my legs and looped over Da's belt, the flaps fell front and back just above my knees. Sheepishly, I went outside trying to look as though I had worn a breechcloth for years, only to find Nipën and an army of women, hands on hips, shaking their heads and tut-tutting – the leather wasn't hanging properly. There was too much at the front and not enough at the back and it was puckered at the waist. It was all they could do not to laugh. Wading in, they straightened the folds and adjusted the belt. I felt a bit of a dunce. Who would have thought wearing a breechcloth would need practice.

It felt strange wearing nothing but a skimpy piece of leather, but as the days went by, I became used to the new garment. In truth, the summer sun had browned my skin so deeply that, from a distance, I looked a little like Mëlëk. Only my chestnut hair revealed I was a white boy. Of course, no self-respecting Native would ever confuse me with one of their own, but to me, the breechcloth seemed like a final camouflage, and I had to 'mind myself that living here wasn't what I truly wanted. My injuries had long since healed and Ireland continued to call me across the ocean. There was no good reason to remain – except for one thing.

Mëlëk had told me of a meeting the previous summer between the Lenape and members of the Council of Philadelphia. A deed, drawn up many years ago in 1686, had been presented to the Lenape, but they doubted the deed was genuine as it hadn't been signed by their ancestors. It declared the Lenape owed land to the Council, but how much land was yet to be decided. Governor Thomas Penn proposed it should be the distance a man could walk in a day and a half, but the chiefs weren't happy with this arrangement, believing the deed to be a forgery.

'If our chief and Governor Penn can agree, will you come with us to observe the walk and help see it is honestly performed?' asked Mëlëk. 'I also fear the white men might show us a document and I cannot read your English word.'

I was happy to oblige, not only because the Lenape had saved my life, but because Mëlëk was as good a friend as any boy ever had. So, it was decided; I would remain with the Lenape a while longer and accompany them to oversee a walk that would decide the amount of hunting ground to be handed over to Thomas Penn. It didn't seem complicated because land was often measured by means of a walk, or sometimes how far a man could ride in a day.

Now that I was taller and stronger, I was invited to join the lessons Kuwèmu gave to all the young men in the art of warfare. Under his instruction, I became skilled in the use of knife and axe. I learned to wrestle, twist a neck, slash behind the knees and overpower an attacker from any side. I was also asked to play *Pahsahëman*. Now, I had kicked a pig's bladder along the lane many times in Ireland, so I reckoned a game of men against women wouldn't be too troublesome. Ha! Those women were fast and strong, and that deerskin ball fair flew around that field! I landed on my rump more often than my feet!

I played alongside a man named Këkëlëksu who was Mëlëk's uncle – his mother's brother. Këkëlëksu seemed to have more importance within the family than Òpalanie; something to do with him being of the same blood as Nipën. He had much of her character too; a happy frame of mind often given to laughter, and thanks to his ability, we won the game! Folk were busy claiming their winnings from the choice of bracelets and beaded necklaces hanging on the bet-string, when suddenly there was a mighty commotion. A woman was screaming. I knew the voice. It was Nipën. Këkëlëksu and Òpalanie tore through the camp to find her, as Mëlëk came running toward me.

'It is Òxehëmu!' he screeched. 'She has been taken!'

A mallet slammed into my heart. *Taken?* Who would do such a thing? Why? Take her where? Frantically collecting our weapons, we joined Kuwèmu, Òpalanie and Këkëlëksu; their crumpled faces grey as grit. We fanned out, searching for tracks. Kuwèmu searched the ground toward the river, while Mëlëk and I scoured the land amongst the trees and Òpalanie and Këkëlëksu examined the earth for that telltale damp leaf upturned as it stuck to a moccasin. Time was everything; every moment was taking Òxehëmu further away. At last, a shout from Këkëlëksu, he had found one of her ribbons lying near a tree.

We tracked her through the forest and over the far hills. She had dropped many items along the way: a painted shell, a bracelet, and even the small beaded ring Mëlëk had made for her. Somehow she'd been sly enough to let the items drift unseen from her hand. Like her brother, she was a canny wee thing.

As the hours passed and the trail veered north-west, I asked Mëlëk why anyone would snatch her. In sombre tones, he explained, 'A child can be taken south and sold as a slave. The plantation owner pay less for a native child than a black slave, who must come from another land. But we follow her north-west, so my father say she will remain with those who have taken her.'

'I don't understand. Why did they take her if not to sell her?'

'A tribe who have lost many of their own people in battle need more female so they can breed and increase in number. She will live with them and someday give the tribe a son or daughter.'

His words coiled around my guts like a snake. There was still so much I didn't understand about this country, so many customs that would be against the law in Ireland.

'We have one small hope,' he continued, 'the young men of a tribe are responsible for stealing children. It help them gain experience without facing battle. If we can find them, we will rescue her with ease.'

I wondered if the Lenape had ever stolen children from other tribes, but didn't ask because, in all honesty, I didn't want to know the answer.

Kuwèmu suddenly halted. 'The trail leads toward Kanadaseaga.'

Këkëlëksu's deep voice rolled on the wind, 'Then we must catch them before nightfall, or tomorrow we will be in their hunting grounds.'

Where was Kanadaseaga? Whose hunting grounds? We continued with as much haste as possible, giving no thought to food or drink, only to finding Òxehëmu. Eventually, from a small hill, we looked down on a river that stretched like a silver thread through a thick, green quilt. Këkëlëksu's words betrayed his desperation, 'If they take to the water we will lose her forever.'

Kuwèmu laid a comforting hand on Këkëlëksu's shoulder. 'Do not despair. A storm is approaching. They will make camp. Then we have them.'

Above us, the pewter sky began to darken like a giant bruise. The wind was rising, moaning like the skirl of Irish pipes. A sudden cry rose above the treetops, 'Ntàpi! ntàpi!' which meant, 'I am here! I am here!' It was Òxehëmu! Knowing we'd be searching for her, she had made as much noise as possible to help us find her. We quickened our pace because she would undoubtedly be punished for her bravery.

As we crept down through the dense foliage to the valley floor, the gathering clouds spat rain upon us with such force, it prickled like nettle-sting. We cared not a jot, but continued stealthily through the dripping vegetation, creeping from tree to tree, until at last, we spied five Natives huddled under the long branches of a sycamore tree. But they were not young. Nor were they inexperienced. Their tattooed bodies revealed years of battle skill. Kuwèmu was rattled. He whispered something about bringing more warriors, but it was too late; we would have to take our chances.

'Menkweyok,' fumed Mëlëk. 'The English call them Senecas.'

I knew of their reputation; they were viciously fierce. The odds of winning against them were overwhelming because although we also numbered five, Mëlëk and I had no battle experience and smallpox had reduced Kuwèmu's weight to such an extent his previous strength hadn't yet returned. The war-chief decided on caution and signalled not to engage in hand-to-hand fighting. Surprise was our best weapon. We would kill with bow, arrow and axe, hopefully without shedding a drop of our own blood.

Òxehëmu was tied by the hands and neck to a young willow tree, sniffing back tears, a bleeding laceration across her cheek where she had been lashed into silence. This sight drew from Këkëlëksu, Kuwèmu and Òpalanie, the nobility of true warriors. They became focused, determined, their expressions set in stone.

Silently we circled the *Menkweyok*, crawling through the undergrowth until positioned and ready, waiting for Kuwèmu's signal. I glanced at Mëlëk – crouched and eager for the slaughter. He had been born to this. I had not. Being brave was not a choice for him, but a way of life. I was a terrified Irish lad from Limavady. I wasn't destined to be a Native warrior, but there was no way out of the situation. All I could do was hope I wouldn't disgrace myself with cowardice.

One of the Seneca stepped a little way into the forest and began to pee against a tree. Kuwèmu was crouched six yards from him. This was too good an opportunity to miss. The tomahawk flew from his hand, cleaving the head of the enemy with a grisly thud. He was a dead man standing. There wasn't even much blood. He simply hit the soaked earth without a sound. A sly grin slithered across Mëlëk's lips. Now there were four.

At any moment Kuwèmu would give the signal. I had to be prepared. Blood throbbed in my head. My fingers gripped my bow so tightly I feared it would snap. A second Seneca rose to his feet and called to his brother who had been absent for too long. Something gleamed on his belt. My eyes narrowed. It was something small: a trinket, a treasure; something unexpectedly familiar. Ma's silver jug!

Shock shuddered through me like the clang of a bell. These were the Natives who had murdered my kin! In an instant, the veil shading my memory melted away. I was back on the ledge. I could see their painted faces, their nose rings and skullcaps coming over the creek toward the settlement. Vomit rose in my throat. Rage flooded through my veins. A tempest of seething hate flowed from every sinew in my body. Ferocious, frenzied madness rose from the pit of my guts! My bow fell to the ground. I drew my knife. No longer aware of anything except the need for revenge, I leapt from the trees like an arrow released, and with a scream, flung myself upon him!

He scarce had time to turn his head in my direction before we toppled into the undergrowth. But rage is no match for experience. His strength was unimaginable. A mighty punch blinded me with blood. The knife flew from my hand. He pinned me to the ground. Seneca spit dripped on my lips. He pressed an arm across my throat. I smashed my fist into his ribs. Momentarily, he lost his grip. I rolled free and struggled to my feet. He kicked the back of my knees. I crashed again to the ground. In a trice, he was on me. I punched and kicked, but he was the weight of a tree. Rotten teeth snarled down at me. Snatching an axe from his belt, he raised the weapon high. I grappled in the mud for something – anything – I could use as a weapon. My fingers touched the handle of my knife. I aimed the blade. With all the force I could muster, I thrust the steel deep under his ribs. A scream of agony rose above the sheeting rain. The axe fell from his hand, but my revenge knew no bounds. I slit his warm hide lengthways. His skin tore open like the fatty rind of a pig. He writhed, blood spurting from his side, then his lifeless, bloody body thudded down on my chest.

Frantically, I wriggled out from under him as though he was diseased. I had been fortunate. I hadn't realised battle could be so ferocious, so barbaric. Everything I'd been taught had flown from my mind in the chaos. My inexperience had almost killed me. Turning on all fours, I heaved vomit, wishing for nothing but to curl into a ball and weep.

Streaks of warm, sticky blood suddenly splattered across my arms. I whirled around, startled by sudden cries. The wet earth was flowing red. A crimson surge of blood gushed from a Seneca neck. His eyes rolled; bloodless moons in a bloodless face. Òpalanie had pole-axed him like a butcher's bull. Këkëlëksu was gutting with precision; unleashing the stench of warm entrails. Mëlëk was slashing with his knife as though he was demented. Screams of pain tore the air. Arms and legs twisted and thrashed. Brutal wounds. Flesh gaping open. Kuwèmu's tomahawk chopped into the chest of the last Seneca warrior, and with that blow – silence.

Breathless, Òpalanie slit the ropes binding Òxehëmu, who leapt into his arms. Mëlëk toppled exhausted to the ground, chest heaving. He was badly injured. They were all injured.

'Mëlëk!' I staggered to my feet, but Kuwèmu blocked my path, his fiery eyes flashing with fury.

'How dare you disobey me!'

'These Natives murdered my kin!' I cried defiantly. 'I have had my revenge!'

But Kuwèmu would not be pacified. 'You need a lesson in obedience, *white boy!*'

It was the only time he ever called me 'white boy', and it stung like a snake bite. They were all staring at me, even Mëlëk. I had been so foolish. Leaping from the bushes had been an unforgivable thing to do. My actions had lost all hope of a surprise attack. I had endangered their lives.

'I-I didn't think…' I stammered, but I could find no words to excuse my conduct and felt the full weight of shame and embarrassment.

Këkëlëksu limped a little way amongst the dripping trees and reappeared with a large handful of dark, wet leaves. Rubbing them to shreds between his palms, he gently patted the mash into the large slash on Mëlëk's leg and the lacerations on his chest and shoulders. He then cut the leggings from one of the Seneca and used the leather to bind Mëlëk's wounds, then attended Kuwèmu and Òpalanie in the same fashion. Finally, he placed the last of the leaves on his own injuries. Struggling to hold back hot tears of disgrace, I cut the silver jug from the belt of the dead Native.

'Are you injured?' Kuwèmu was addressing me, his eyes still bright with anger.

'I-I'm unhurt,' I faltered, my eyes fixed on the ground.

Turning toward the others, he announced flatly, 'We must leave. It is a long way home. Mëlëk, rip our arrows from the bodies of the *Menkweyok*. We must take every weapon with us. They belong to the six nation confederacy, and we do not want trouble with them over this.'

As the rain eased, we walked the long path back to camp in silence. Even Òxehëmu, safe in Òpalanie's arms, remained silent. Kuwèmu was limping badly, and I realised the battle had sapped every bit of his strength. I stayed at the rear, wet and shivering with cold, not wanting to meet eyes with anyone, not even Mëlëk. I thought the day I avenged my da and ma would be the best day of my life, but I arrived back at camp humiliated and scorned.

In the following days, I kept myself apart and talked to no one because I knew the whole camp had heard of my foolishness. Mëlëk was also quiet, and for the first time since the day of my arrival, I was unsure what to say to him. We didn't go hunting together because his wounds needed healing, so I hunted alone, glad of my own company. Sometimes I felt so awkward back in the *wikëwam*, I stayed in the forest until nightfall.

Then late one evening when we both should have been asleep, I heard his voice beside me, 'I will hunt tomorrow. Will you come with me?'

I reckon he was like me: staring into the blackness, wondering how to make things right between us.

'I'll be glad to go with you, Mëlëk.'

But those few words were not enough for me. My shame and remorse tumbled like tallow down a candle, coiling in a hard lump around my heart, leaving me rigid, rooted in regret. 'Forgive me, Mëlëk!' I blurted. 'Such a rage took hold of me, I lost all reason. I didn't mean to put you in danger!'

He made no reply and I feared I would never be pardoned, then suddenly he chirped, 'Kuwèmu said you fought well, and when you are older you will be a fierce opponent.'

I could scarce believe his words. 'Kuwèmu said that – of me? But he hates me!'

'He does not hate you. He was shocked to find *Menkweyok* warrior. He hoped for a younger enemy. When my father and Këkëlëksu saw Òxehëmu tied and bleeding, their fury was as strong as your need for revenge. We understand more than you think. Do not be sad. We have survived – and are wiser for it.'

I settled down under the fur cover. I couldn't see his smile, but I could hear it in his voice and knew we were, and always would be, the very best of brothers.

THE DECEIT OF THOMAS PENN

Gradually, the days grew shorter. The sleepy earth yawned; its moist, misty breath hanging motionless in the cold morning air as a quiet weariness settled over the land. The swallows flew away, and we glimpsed the first red-tinged leaves of autumn. A year had passed since I lost my kin, and somewhere along the way, the young boy who witnessed that terrible slaughter had also been lost, though not by sudden misfortune. He had quietly drifted away like an anchorless boat until he was only a speck on the horizon, and I stood firmly in his place; older, stronger and more acquainted with the ways of life.

Despite my ill-timed attack on the Seneca, the fight had released me from guilt, slipping from my shoulders where it had clung for a twelve month. At last, I was wise enough to realise nothing could have saved my kin, least of all a small boy. The silver jug now hung on *my* belt, a constant reminder I had done everything possible to avenge their deaths.

While women were busy with the bean harvest, the men hunted in earnest. Everyone was occupied laying up food for the winter. Mëlëk told me a great ceremony called *Gamwing* would take place after the harvest, to thank the Creator. I reckoned it would be like Harvest Thanksgiving at Derry Church, except the Lenape feasted for twelve days, whereas we considered ourselves right fortunate to have enough food for one good meal.

On a cold afternoon, as children were cutting rings of pumpkin and threading them over sticks to dry by the fires, Mëlëk announced, 'Aihàmtët, the time for the walk has arrived. Thomas Penn and a man named Logan met with our four chief during *Winaminke Kishux* – your month of August. A man called Barefoot Brinston translated. Our chief were shown a map of the walk and have agreed upon it. Three of our tribe – Neepaheilomon, his brother in marriage, Tom, and another man named John Combush – will also attend. Neepaheilomon speak English like me. We will leave tomorrow and journey to a place called Wrightstown.'

This information should have pleased me. After the walk, I could search for work in Philadelphia and someday find a ship to take me home. Yet, I knew my life would be forever affected by these people. When I was once again on Irish soil and walking through fields of golden flax along the Roe Valley where the linnets sing, I knew there would be a sense of absence, of loss, and the thought of it made my heart ache.

We were small in number: Chief Lapowinsa, John Combush, Neepaheilomon, Tom, Mëlëk and me. Why Tom and John Combush had English names, I could not say, but I liked them immediately. They had a reputation as strong warriors, yet they also enjoyed a bit of devilment, like a couple of changelings put on this good earth for the sole purpose of causing mischief.

With only three horses, including Samson, we doubled up – two riders to one horse – and made good time. Fording a creek called Karakung, we crossed land named Chingsessing, then a wide, deep river, using canoes left at either side for whoever had need of them, while the horses swam alongside. When the sun was high, we caught a young turkey, pulled some cattails and enjoyed a good meal, and by late evening, set camp on the outskirts of Wrightstown.

Settled around the evening fire, all conversation turned to the approaching walk.

'How much ground will they cover?' asked Mëlëk.

Chief Lapowinsa shrugged. 'Perhaps twenty miles. They will catch something to eat, light a fire and cook the meat as we do, then rest and smoke some tobacco before continuing the walk.'

John Combush, who had been scouting the area and familiarising himself with the land, reappeared, looking concerned.

'Chief Lapowinsa, I have discovered a path has been cleared for the walkers so they will not waste time jumping over fallen branches or searching for the right direction. Some trees have even been blazed and cleared. I have also learned the path does not follow the *Lenapewihittuk* as it should, but moves inland, and the men who are to walk have been promised money and land if they do well.'

'Mëlëk, what is the *Lenapewihittuk*?' I whispered.

'It is the river you call the Delaware.'

I watched a grey shadow of uneasiness settle on Chief Lapowinsa's face. Something threatening had crept over us. We all sensed it. In his hand he held a small, crude, crumpled map of the walk and Neepaheilomon suddenly stared at the boundary lines and asked, 'Chief Lapowinsa, who gave you this map?'

'A man called Hamilton at our last meeting with Thomas Penn.'

Neepaheilomon pointed to a river marked on the parchment. 'That river cannot be Tohickon Creek. I believe it is the *Lechauwekink* which is a much greater distance from Wrightstown.'

The chief held the map toward the firelight and studied the lines. 'You see well, Neepaheilomon. They mean to confuse us.'

'Confuse us?' queried Mëlëk in alarm. 'What can we do?'

'Nothing.' It was a simple reply. Chief Lapowinsa rarely wasted words. 'I know not the workings of the white mind, but the agreement must be honoured. We will discover tomorrow if they have taken us for fools. It is late. The walk begins at dawn. We must sleep.'

Wrapped in skins, we sat around the fire, a breeze ambling through the sassafras trees and the whole, wide starry heaven above our heads. The walk felt like an axe ready to fall across our necks, yet we couldn't understand how they planned to deceive us.

We roused ourselves when everything was still shadowy and quiet. Mëlëk and I rekindled the fire, then we all ate hot corn gruel – or *sapàn* as the Lenape called it – followed by cold turkey meat and white cedar tea with sweet *sëpi shukël*. All too soon, dawn tugged away the frayed edges of night and we made our way along a narrow path to Wrightstown.

The starting point of the walk was a large chestnut tree which stood in the centre of the small town, and even though the hour was early, a grand crowd of white folk had gathered, including many settlers who had scrubbed up well for the occasion.

We discovered the walkers were called Solomon Jennings, James Yeates and Edward Marshall. They cut three fine figures. Young, strong and muscular, they paced around like caged bears. The observers for Thomas Penn were called Chapman, Eastburn, Scull and Steele, while the official observers for the Lenape were Neepaheilomon, Tom and John Combush. The timekeeper was a sheriff by the name of Timothy Smith, a proud-looking man with what I can only describe as an unfortunate face. He had the hooked mouth of a salmon at breeding time; his under-jaw jutting further out than his top lip, which gave the impression of a constant snarl.

Each walker placed a hand on the ridged bark of the chestnut tree. Anticipation hushed all voices. Silence settled on eager, expectant faces. Sheriff Smith held high his kerchief and studied his pocket watch. Suddenly, with a flourish of his fingers, the blue cotton fluttered to the ground. Cheers erupted from the crowd as the men set off, but their speed could hardly be called walking! They ran as though they had been poured along that path from a bucket! What joukery-pawkery! What trickery! This was hardly fair! Chief Lapowinsa paled. Mëlëk threw up his hands in disgust, but no one paid heed to our cries of complaint. We may as well have been invisible.

Neepaheilomon, Tom and John Combush sprinted after them, while Chief Lapowinsa, Mëlëk and I followed on horseback. The path had indeed been cleared, as though some poor maidservant, with bonnet and broom, had swept her way along it. Soon the crowd fell far behind, with only those on horseback able to match the speed of the walkers. Long legs stretching and shirts billowing, they hurtled through forest and streams, their drenched leather shoes slapping like wet fish and breeches drying in the breeze. Surely they couldn't continue this pace for long!

Pink-faced, they passed a lodging house called *The Gardenville* where a servant carrying logs stopped and stared at the sight. Chief Lapowinsa suddenly halted; his face grey as winter. 'I will have no more of this deception! They make a mockery of us and the law! How could we have been so unguarded?!' In ten miles he had aged ten years. Angrily, he turned his horse toward a different trail.

'Where is he bound?' I queried, because I could see no dwellings.

'To Hockendauqua,' replied Mëlëk. 'It is a Lenape village. He live there with Chief Tishcohen.'

I watched that great chief, hunched like a dog in the rain, disappear through tumbling autumn leaves toward his home, the anguish of self-reproach hanging about him like a mourning garment.

Galloping after Neepaheilomon and the others, we rounded a bend to find someone on the ground. It was the walker, Solomon Jennings. Sheriff Smith was kneeling beside him, tending the stricken man. Jennings was ash-grey and sweating like a stuck pig, not a dry thread on his body. He could die for all I cared. It was the sheriff I wanted to confront because he represented the law and was the one person who could put an end to this farce. I slid down from the saddle, but laying eyes on my breechcloth, he mistook me for a Native and took a cautious step backwards.

'Sheriff Smith!' I seethed. 'How can you allow such barefaced deception?'

When he heard my speak, he realised his error. His fish mouth widened to a sneer of contempt and he regarded me in surprise. 'Well, I see we got us a turncoat – a white boy in the 'guise of an Injun! So, you've forsaken your own people and sided with these savages!' In his stupidity, it hadn't occurred to him that Mëlëk might understand every word.

I tried not to let it rankle. 'The Lenape are *not* savages! They signed the agreement in good faith the walk would be honestly performed! You are a sheriff bound by law to see this walk is fair! Have you no shame?'

He seemed incredulous that I should address him in such a manner.

'You young whelp! You wear the clothes of an Injun, yet talk to *me* of shame!'

'I'm ashamed of none but folk like you!' I exclaimed. 'The walk should follow the Delaware and be a walk – not a run!'

That vile man drew close – too close. I could see pus-filled, white-headed pimples on his greasy-skinned neck. 'This walk has been in the plannin' for two years!' he menaced. 'They race for land and money! What care I if the Lenape lose every tree and river? Thomas Penn is deep in debt and there are plenty of settlers waitin' to pay handsomely for such land!'

'*Two year!*' cried Mëlëk.

The sheriff couldn't have looked more shocked if someone had placed the barrel of a musket in his mouth.

'You have been planning to cheat the Lenape for *two year*!'

Pulling his knife from his belt, Mëlëk leapt from his horse, but I quickly blocked his path. Angrily, he pushed against me, knife raised, but I held my footing. 'Hold, Mëlëk! This is not a day for murder! Come now, let us not waste a moment more on this scum!'

Grudgingly, he sheathed his knife then spat two final words at the sheriff, 'Eat crow!'

I knew that was an insult because crow is the worst-tasting bird on God's good earth.

The remainder of that day was dismal. Every hour measured in miles, and every mile measured in anguish. Neepaheilomon, John Combush and Tom eventually rode with us because the pace of the walkers was perilous. Yeates and Marshall ran past Tohickon Creek, which we understood to be the boundary, resting only a few moments to drink and eat a little nourishment, before continuing at the same pace. Eventually, Sheriff Smith signalled the end of the walk for that day. By then it was six of the clock. Those men had run for twelve hours and Neepaheilomon reckoned they had covered more than forty miles.

As it happened, Yeates and Marshall had halted at a place near Hockendauqua Creek – half a mile from Chief Lapowinsa's village. Sheriff Smith, now armed with a musket, scowled at us. 'Let not any man trouble me or these walkers while they sleep! Be warned, I will happily blast your brains into next week should the need arise!'

Despite his threats, he had to employ armed guards to protect the two men, knowing every Native in the area wanted to kill them.

At the village of Hockendauqua, we found Chief Nutimus and Chief Manawkyhickon had arrived, eager for news of the walk. Chief Nutimus was already in his eighty-sixth year; the wrinkles on his face like ripples of wet sand, but his eyes were bright and clear. Neepaheilomon related the day's events to the four chiefs – Chief Tishcohen also being present as Hockendauqua was his home. The whole village then vented their anger with shouts and cries of indignation at being treated so disgracefully. The day had been more woeful than any of us could have imagined, and I wondered how far this dark deed would carry down the coming years. One thing was certain; it wouldn't be easily forgotten.

Early morning tiptoed past leaving rain enough for a paddle; a grey day to match our grey mood. Mëlëk and I lay by a fire that had long since given up its flame. We were supposed to observe the second day of the walk, but were so dispirited we made not the slightest effort to attend. Eventually, the observers for Penn nervously came to the camp to ask why we hadn't arrived.

'The walk is unlawful!' cried Chief Lapowinsa.

Neepaheilamon, in an effort to calm the situation, addressed the chiefs, 'With your permission, Mëlëk, Aihàmtët and I will attend the walk so they will not say we conceded in silence, but rebuked them until the very last step.'

Chief Nutimus nodded in agreement, then wrapping his mantel around his shoulders, bent his head in resignation, like the slow, silent tumble of an old tombstone.

We arrived wet and cold at the starting point. Marshall and Yeates set off again at that same swift pace along a path that became ever more mountainous. Yeates, corpse grey, seemed unsure in which direction the path lay and often stumbled until, coming to a creek, he lurched waist-deep into the flow and sank beneath the water. Before observers could rescue him, Marshall turned back and pulled him to the bank where Yeates lay gasping and screaming he was blind. How could a man run himself blind? Whatever the cause, I had little sympathy for him.

Marshall ran onward, finally toppling at the appointed hour near a place called Mauch Chunk. How much ground he had covered over the day and a half we couldn't tell, although there was talk he'd run more than sixty miles. But the real devil in all of this was surely Thomas Penn. Guilty of falsehoods, outrageous mischief and deception, I wished with all my heart I could see him hanging from a gibbet.

SHACKAMAXON

I remained quiet, minding my tongue while rage bubbled around me. In truth, I tried to keep my head down, afeared I might be thrown from the camp simply for having the same colour skin as those walkers.

The chiefs smouldered with fury, remembering the good faith they had enjoyed with Thomas Penn's father, William Penn, by all accounts a fair and righteous man they called Brother Onas. I reckon that poor man must have turned in his grave with shame at the antics of his son.

Chief Lapowinsa sent Neepehailomon, Tom and John Combush to the Lenape villages of Arronemink and Nittabakonk to tell them what had happened and of the expected loss of land. The inhabitants of those villages would then carry the bad tidings to other Lenape villages.

Now, I can't say by what means Marshall returned to his home, but I did hear a snippet of interesting information about Sheriff Smith. He was only a few miles from his home town when he was set upon by three Natives who almost beat the life out of him. At least that was the rumour and it pleased me to believe it. I think Neepehailomon, Tom and John Combush devised brave punishment for that sheriff because he did nothing to prevent the injustice of the walk.

One of the observers, Benjamin Eastburn, was also the surveyor general. It was his task to measure the land covered by the walk and we were to wait on him at Philadelphia to hear the final calculations. Mëlëk was silent for most of that solemn journey. In truth, there was little speak from anyone. Discouraged and depressed, the four chiefs, Mëlëk and I trudged slowly south for three days, barely covering ten miles a day until, at last, we arrived at a place called Shackamaxon, which lay near the Delaware River and was well known to the Lenape. I was heartsore for my friend and tried to think of a way to raise his spirits.

'Mëlëk, how near are we to Philadelphia?'

'It is a short walk through the forest. Why do you ask?'

'Have you ever seen the town or the port where the ships dock?'

He soberly shook his head. 'I have been to Philadelphia with my father and the Elder, but I have not seen the port.'

'Then let us go there directly,' I encouraged. 'I would like to show you where I first laid eyes on this land and the great ships that sail the ocean!'

'Is there not *tëspehëleokàn* in the town?' Since Kuwèmu had been ill, we were all much more aware of smallpox.

'I overheard settlers at Wrightstown say the outbreak of last year has almost disappeared,' I replied. In truth, I had overheard more than that. It seemed a man called Benjamin Franklin, a clerk for the general assembly, had lost his four-year-old son to smallpox. Perhaps there were two men of that name. If not, then I was truly sorry for that kind man.

Roused by my enthusiasm, we promised the chiefs we would return by sunset. At last, I would see the sights of Philadelphia.

By the time we crossed Vine Street, the sickly stench of urine from the tanneries was already bristling in our nostrils, and by High Street, we were in the thick of the bustling town. Peddlers darted between carriages and clattering carts, dodging the horse dung and calling out their wares. Hollow-cheeked young girls in stained pinners were selling nuts, flowers and eggs. Charcoal merchants heaved heavy handcarts, women were selling scarves and shawls and a baker shouted after a young lad who was stuffing the evidence of his crime swiftly into his mouth as he ran. Hucksters were carrying wicker crates crammed with squawking fowl while an old man in even older clothes was playing the fiddle for a few coins.

Chestnut Street was just as lively. We peeped through open doorways where carvers, carpenters and joiners plied their trade. Noisy forging shops blackened the air with soot. A shoemaker sat at a bench scattered with pieces of leather, hammers, dyes and cutters. Curly snuff horns, combs, drinking horns, buttons, lantern panes and finely polished powder horns were displayed in the window of a master Horner. The smell of burnt bones drifted from a workshop where a pot of thick bone glue sat on a warm stove and a young man, surrounded by wood shavings, worked a small treadle lathe, just like the chair bodgers in Ireland. We even saw the state house, which didn't look quite finished, but still would have been difficult to miss because from end to end it was longer than the entire main street of Limavady.

Wherever we went, heads turned to look at us. Some folk even crossed to the other side of the street to avoid us. Perhaps breechcloths weren't a common sight in the town. Or maybe we shouldn't have carried our knives.

As we passed the shop of Peter Stretch, a watchmaker on the corner of Front and Chestnut Street, Mëlëk pointed with astonishment at the tall masts and spars he could already see towering above the rooftops. A few moments later, we gazed upon the sun-drenched port. The day's catch had long since been sold and the fishing boats, some baked pale by the heat and others barnacled like a skin disease, bobbed in the shadow of majestic, graceful, tall ships – the proud old ladies of the sea. Mëlëk was staggered by their size. Until that moment, he had seen nothing larger than a canoe, and I could only watch, amused by his astonished expression, as he realised the mighty trees he chopped for firewood could also be used to build these magnificent beasts of the sea.

'If you could only see them in full sail! They are indeed a sight to behold!' I cried.

He gaped at the size and strength of the tar-slapped boards, marvelling at their structure. How many souls did they carry? What provision was there for fresh water? Where did folk sleep? What were the names of the masts and the many sails? It was fortunate I'd paid attention to the lessons on the outward journey! Mëlëk had known nothing of these ships, and it pleased me greatly that, at last, he was able to catch a glimpse of my world.

A pilot boat was guiding a large square-rigger toward the port. The battered ship, sails now furled and flying an English ensign, looked as though it had weathered a good many storms. We watched in silence as it docked at the Penn landing stage and the Collector of Duties went aboard. Soon, folk barely able to stand for lack of food spilled unsteadily across the gangplank, as we had done not three years since. Immigrants. Before they had even set their worn shoes on solid ground, they were the enemy, detested by every tribe. They all desired land, and Thomas Penn was the man to give it to them by whatever means necessary. Our spirits suddenly deflated, we turned to leave, but a small, wizened sailor, brown as a penny and sitting on a wall in the sun taking his ease, caught my attention. I knew that face! 'Scuttle-Butt Bill!' I called. 'Good day to you!'

Shading his eyes, he looked up at me, but being taller and wearing a breechcloth, didn't recognise me, even though it was plain by my speech I was no Native. He rose cautiously to his feet. I offered my hand, which he shook with a certain amount of hesitation; unable to place me amongst the hundreds of immigrants he'd helped transport across the ocean.

'You 'ave me at a disadvantage, young man,' he said, a note of suspicion in his voice.

'My name is William – William Baxter.' It was the first time in a year I had heard my English name. 'And this is my friend, Mëlëk.' He gave a short nod to Mëlëk by way of a greeting, and I liked him all the better for it. Plenty of white folk wouldn't acknowledge a Native. 'My kin had passage under Captain Liston from Derry to this very port not three years ago, and vastly entertained we were with yer tales!'

His entire countenance suddenly brightened. 'Indeed, sir! I mind you now! You wur full o' questions! Well! You 'ave growed! You 'ad a brother – John. No, James?'

I felt my heart lurch. 'I did, but he's no longer of this world.' I briefly dropped my gaze to the ground.

'I'm sorry to 'ear that, young master, but it's a common enough thing in this land. Many 'ave trod the same path,' he sighed.

I had no desire to say more on the subject, so asked instead, 'Scuttle-Butt, have you newly arrived from Ireland?'

'Lord no, Master William. We been docked a good week or better but been occupied wi' repairs.' The sound of hammering and the scritch-scratch of a saw echoed across the port as he pointed toward a ship docked far to the right. The *Mary*! With so many ships, I hadn't noticed her! 'We wus damaged in a gale, but she will soon be worthy. This is 'urricane season, but we will take our chance. We sail wi' the tide in six days.'

'Are you bound for Derry?' I asked with a glimmer of hope.

'No, we sail for Béal Feirste.'

Béal Feirste! A few days' walk around the Antrim Coast would see me home! I glanced at the silver jug hanging on my belt. It was so precious to me; the only possession I had to remind me of Ma, but if I didn't sell it, I faced years of servitude until I had money enough for the journey.

'Have you passage for one more soul?' I asked eagerly.

'We do, sir, because we return wi' only cargo; flaxseed an' tobacco.'

'Then I may sail with you?'

'I'll speak to the captain, but I see no reason why you should not return wi' us. The evenin' tide in six days, mind! We cannot wait!'

I had seen a shop in the town that belonged to a silversmith and told Mëlëk of my plan. Hurriedly retracing our steps to High Street, we found the blue-painted sign of *Silversmith Elias Boudinot*. Mëlëk chose to wait outside, uncertain if it was acceptable for Natives to enter a white man's shop.

Inside was all glitter and gleam. Silver rings, bracelets, brooches, spoons, tea and coffee pots, jugs, plates and candlesticks decorated the shelves. I hailed the shopkeeper; a small, balding man, who peered at me over the rim of his thin spectacles. Knowing he may take fright at the sight of my breechcloth, I quickly explained I was Irish, and had silver to sell if he was in the market to buy. He eagerly rubbed his hands and asked, 'Well now, young man, what have you?'

Slipping the jug from my belt, I laid it before him. Such an instant change of expression I have rarely seen on any man. His gnarled hands caressed that silver as though it was the most precious thing in the world. First, he gently rubbed it with a cloth, then held a small glass to one eye, as though searching for something, then finally laid the jug on the bench and exclaimed, 'I am indeed in the market for buying. This piece has a DK stamp.'

'DK?' It meant nothing to me.

'It's the mark of David King, a silversmith from Dublin; a master silver and goldsmith to be precise. Indeed, by the shape and design, I would judge it to be one of his early pieces, from about 1695.' His eyes suddenly narrowed. 'How came you in possession of such a fine piece?'

'It belonged to my ma. I got no further knowledge of it, sir.'

Leaning toward me, he lowered his voice and said sternly, 'Hearken well to me, young man, did you come by this little jug dishonestly?'

I drew back, affronted. 'You think because I wear the garments of a Native, I must be a thief? My kin were murdered! That silver jug is the only possession I got to remind me of my ma, and now I am forced to part with it to pay for passage home!'

At my outburst, he raised his hands and became altogether more agreeable. 'Calm yourself, young sir! I have no desire to offend, but we are a reputable establishment. The goods I receive must be honestly acquired,' he stated firmly.

'I can assure you, sir, the jug is mine by right!'

This seemed proof enough because he placed the jug on his scales and carefully weighed it. 'I trust you are not going to pay me in wampum, sir?'

Wampum was Native money; six beads made a stiver, and twenty stivers made a guilder, which was near enough a sixpence.

'We do not deal in wampum!' he exclaimed. 'We pay in Spanish dollars, and you are fortunate I am an honest man and will pay you the true value!' Unlocking a drawer below his bench, he grasped an abundance of coins and dropped them in my sweaty palm. I had never before laid eyes on such riches!

'Thank you, sir! This will pay for passage home and a good deal more besides!' Grabbing his hand, I shook it as though I was flapping washing, then placed the jangling coins safely in the pouch around my waist and joined Mëlëk outside in the sunshine.

'I am happy for you, brother.' He smiled, but his words were tinged with just the slightest hesitation and I knew, as he did, that saying farewell was going to be painful for us both.

I was in need of clothes for the journey and obliged to buy them before I departed because, once back in Ireland, I couldn't use Spanish dollars. Having set aside the money for passage, I decided to spend every last coin and within the hour, had bought a linen shirt, breeches, woollen leggings and a pair of stout boots. I now had a mind to buy some treats with the remaining pieces of eight.

'What meats shall we purchase? Mëlëk, have you ever tasted dumplings?' My mouth watered at the very thought of them. He had little time to reply because I grabbed his arm and we scampered through the streets, returning to Shackamaxon before dark with all kinds of delicious nourishment: dried beef, boiled dumplings, muffins, cinnamon buns, bread, pot pies and a small loaf of something called scrapple.

Now, nothing in the world would have lifted the spirits of the Lenape that evening, but that food proved a small distraction. They had a sup of everything. Chief Lapowinsa ate an entire pot pie, declaring it a tasty meal, while we described all the diversions of the town, and I explained I'd found a ship to take me home. As twilight turned to darkness, we grew silent around the crackling fire, everyone thinking on the morrow; the day we would discover how much land had been lost to Thomas Penn as a result of the walk. To the Lenape, land meant food and warmth – wood for fires and animals to hunt. If Edward Marshall had indeed covered sixty miles, the area lost could measure several hundred square miles. To lose such an amount was unthinkable.

An arrow suddenly whooshed over the flames and thudded into the earth behind us. It was the last thing I expected. I leapt to my feet, knife in hand, ready for a fight! Mëlëk patiently pulled my arm and entreated me to sit. 'Still you have not learned who dip his arrow in bloodroot!' His diamond eyes danced with teasing delight as the rustle of mantles against leafy branches stirred the night air, and dark figures emerged from the trees.

Kuwèmu and the warriors were welcomed to the fire.

BETRAYAL

Grandma told me that every person has a spirit, and every spirit has a colour. She could see those colours; shades of calm blues, or happy yellows, or fiery-tempered reds. She said young folk were a whirl of colours because their spirit hadn't yet settled. Others were dull and faded like old drapes, or shone so brightly it made her squint. But there was one colour she warned me about; the colour of evil. It was black as a cauldron and latched onto anyone who desired it; feeding on anger and greed, and leaving the stench of ruin in its wake. Remembering her words, I wished with all my heart she had met Thomas Penn because then I would have known the depth of his darkness and could have warned the Lenape.

We crowded into a large room simply furnished with benches and one long table. In what building, I couldn't say because I simply followed Mëlëk, but there were no drapes at the windows or comfort of any kind. Even Grandma, poor as she was, had a sack of feathers to cushion her rump.

Present were the four chiefs, Kuwèmu, the warriors, Mëlëk and me. Taking our places at the far side of the table, we faced a host of white faces: Eastburn, a man named Richard Peters, Conrad

145

Weiser the interpreter, and hovering like hawks, the handful of men who had carried ale and food for the walkers to help them overcome their exhaustion; a shameful deed. The guards who had protected the walkers were also present; muskets loaded. They unnerved me. What possible reason could they have for attending the meeting?

I barely had time to warm the seat when all present fell silent. A gentleman dressed in great finery – a grey, knee-length satin coat, matching waistcoat and breeches, white silk stockings and a curled wig upon his head – entered the room. With a parchment rolled under one arm, he sauntered arrogantly to the table. I never thought to lay eyes on Governor Thomas Penn, yet there he was, not ten feet from me. Without welcoming the Lenape, or looking them in the eye, he got straight down to business. I sensed immediately he was a different creature; moulded by some other hand.

The parchment, a map of Penn's country, was unrolled on the table. We crowded around, holding down the tattered edges as Conrad Weiser studied the new boundary line. I'd heard Weiser had been raised by the Mohawk and was highly esteemed and trusted by many tribes, so was surprised to see him frown. He was troubled. Something was amiss. He glanced at Eastburn. A whispered discussion began, and I quickly understood the boundary hadn't been drawn as expected but rose many miles to the north-east. Mëlëk glanced at me in confusion, unable to grasp their hushed, heated words. I had no knowledge of where the boundary *should* have been because I did not know the towns or rivers, however, from my position at the table, I could see a large swirl of letters, written by a fine hand across the bottom of the parchment. Leaning forward, I examined the writing. First, the date of the walk was mentioned:

The day of our Lord 19th September 1737.

This was followed by the name of the surveyor general, the measurements of various parcels of ground and a list of signatures, including that of Thomas Penn. My eyes roamed further down, searching for the all-important quantity of land.

What mischief was this?!

I could barely comprehend the amount!

Surely there had been a miscalculation!

One thousand two hundred square miles, equal to seven hundred and sixty-eight thousand acres.

The number fell from my lips in a stunned whisper.

Beside me, Mëlëk heard my words. A flush of crimson fury seeped across his cheeks. He gaped at me, wide-eyed as a newborn calf, then whirling toward the chiefs, spat out the dreaded news! Shock hit the Lenape like cannon fire, vibrating right through them, blowing apart their hopes. No one moved, yet the room quivered with a silence deep as the years. They glared at the sly predator, waiting to hear him deny the scandalous deception, but Penn the parasite spoke not one word, and so the jaws of greed snapped shut upon the Lenape.

Uproar! The table was overturned! Chairs and benches were flung across the room as Kuwèmu's wrath raged above the sound of splintering wood, 'We have been caught in a white man's trap!' he screeched. 'He has blunted the beak of the Lenape! He has ripped out our wings! He has blinded our eyes and pulled out our claws!' A white-knuckled fist punched the air. 'But I am Kuwèmu! War-Chief of the Lenape! And I will make the white man suffer for this treachery!'

I was trembling. The depth and ferocity of Kuwèmu's anger frightened me. If fury had been a living beast, he would have torn every white man in that room to shreds. Guards shielded Penn and Eastburn. Weiser snatched the parchment, and that entire, despicable company of men fled for the door!

We returned to Shackamaxon, stunned by the loss of land. Kuwèmu's eyes betrayed a dark turn of mind. He and the warriors pulled a bloodroot plant, then worked with quiet purpose; cutting, soaking and boiling the roots. When the dye was prepared, they painted their skin deep sunset red. I had never seen a Lenape warrior painted for battle until that moment and was heartily glad I wasn't their enemy.

'We will meet again at the settlement.' They were the only words Kuwèmu spoke and his tone assured us there would be no discussion. He simply led his warriors quietly away through the trees. Without his protective force I felt insecure and unsettled, but soon debate on the walk was all-consuming, and eventually, there was little time to wonder where he'd gone, or when he would return.

'I refuse to leave this land!' thundered Chief Nutimus. 'I will not fall prey to their cheating!' He stormed around the remains of the night fire, whirling this way and that in fury. 'There is only one thing to do. We must inform the Haudenosaunee of what has befallen us and ask for their help!'

'We will not *need* to inform them!' scorned Chief Lapowinsa. 'Mëlëk and Aihàmtët have discovered Penn had been planning the walk for two years! I believe the Haudenosaunee have been well aware of the deception from the very beginning! Penn will have guarded his allegiance to them by promising them a portion of our lost land. The Haudenosaunee have simply been biding their time until this day.'

Silence as thick as mud seeped over our small party as everyone tried to make sense of what had happened. I had no understanding of the politics of their situation and asked Mëlëk why the Haudenosaunee would plot with Penn against the Lenape?

'Many year ago, before I was born, the Lenape fought the Haudenosaunee in battle. The Lenape were defeated. We are a conquered people – a thorn in the flesh of the Haudenosaunee. We are hated by them and forbidden to make any decision without their permission.'

Now I understood what a dreadful predicament this was for the Lenape. The Haudenosaunee would be delighted at their plight and there was no help from any other quarter.

Chief Lapowinsa's eyes suddenly blazed. 'Listen to me, brothers! We will do as the Cherokee have done! Do you not remember? They sent a delegation of seven men to the land of King George! The Warrior Chief Oukah Ulah accompanied them. So did Attakullakulla and Kallannah. They remained for more than a season and presented the king with a crown of eagle feathers and four scalps! There was not a tribe in the land who did not hear of their visit! Why do *we* not also make that journey? We will inform the King of England what deceivers his subjects are and ask for his help! Surely he will heed our distress!'

'We cannot do as the Cherokee have done!' Chief Nutimus responded wearily. 'They were accompanied by a white man who was acquainted with the king and who paid for their journey. We have neither white man's coins, nor an introduction to the king!'

Cherokee Natives walking the streets of London? I could scarce believe it. 'Mëlëk, the *Cherokee* went to *England?*'

'It is true. Seven summer have passed since the Cherokee went to the land of King George with a white man. Many season ago, three Mohawk and one Mohican also crossed the great water to that land. The Sachem of the Mohegan – Mahomet Weyonomon – also travelled to the land of King George. But he died there. I would not want to die so far from my home.'

As I tried to absorb this astonishing information, a sudden thought began to muddle around in my head. If the Lenape couldn't journey across the ocean to beg for help, I could write of their plight and take the letter with me – not to England because I knew full well I had no hope of being granted an audience with the king, but to Ireland, where a man of great importance called the sovereign lived. The position of sovereign had been granted by no less than the king himself, so if anyone knew how a letter might be delivered to the king, it would be him. I whispered this plan to Mëlëk.

'Are you acquainted with this man?' A fragile hope kindled in his eyes.

'The sovereign wouldn't stoop to parley with a ragamuffin like me,' I admitted, 'but I know of him because my grandma told me that when she was a girl, every butcher who slaughtered a cow was obliged, by law, to give the tongue to the sovereign. He is a man of great importance and lives in Béal Feirste. Did Scuttle-Butt not say the ship sails for that town? I will seek him out and beg audience – you may depend upon it!'

When Mëlëk explained my plan to the chiefs, a glimmer of light broke into their darkness. With great excitement, they began to prepare. 'We will barter tobacco for parchment, ink and quill from a trader who lives near the waters of the Muckinipattis,' declared Chief Tishcohen, 'and when we are again at the settlement, Aihàmtët can write of our grievances!' Leaving them eagerly discussing the letter, we walked through the trees to the river where it was quiet and peaceful. I dipped my feet in the cold, dark water, while Mëlëk lay on the cool grass, folded his arms behind his head, as was his habit, and closed his eyes. The ragged head of a kingfisher flashed blue among overhanging branches, and four young moorhens with their telltale red beaks, dally-dawdled around in the cool of the afternoon.

Mëlëk opened one eye and murmured, 'Aihàmtët, tell me of your country and the place you were born.'

The question caught me a mite off balance. I'd been in this land so long it took a few moments to draw images of Ireland to mind.

'I lived in a small house made of stone in the village of Newtown-Limavady, about ten miles from the ocean,' I began, my mind drifting back to the place I called home. 'It was a fair bustling wee place, with shoemakers, skinners, saddlers, carpenters and thatchers. It lies not far from the town of Londonderry, with its thick, stone walls to protect it from raiders. Derry is always lively, much like Philadelphia, but I preferred the hills. In spring the valleys are covered in yellow gorse, and in summer, purple heather flows from Sawel to Slieve Gallion. I would climb the slopes of Binevenagh, or spend days jumping silver streams rich with fish when I should have been working with my da – and had a belting more than once for my trouble! The day I left my homeland, I stood on the deck and watched Binevenagh slowly disappear over the horizon.'

'I understand why you want to go home. Your country is peaceful. It is a good place to live.'

I shook my head. 'If I have learned one thing, Mëlëk, it's this: there is no such place as a peaceful land. There is no New World. There are problems in Ireland as there are here. Both countries are full of hardship.' I lay on my back beside him. 'I'll tell you this, though, when I return to Ireland, I'm going to build a cabin like the one I built with Da, and lay within it all my treasures from this life. On the back wall, I'll hang my prayer stick and my hunting bow and arrows, then I'll fashion bracelets and necklaces as the Lenape do, with shells; cockles, black mussels, white-tipped limpets, silver razor shells and curly brown periwinkles. I may even wear my breechcloth and scare the life out of the folk of Limavady.'

We lay breathing in the soft silence. A fish snapped the surface of the water, and soon those small eventide flies that like to bite and itch began to gather. I could hear distant voices, but curiously the sound was not coming from the direction of our camp. Rolling on my belly, I stretched my head above the grass. Far along the riverbank, an army of Natives was coming toward us; women carrying bairns in backboards and men in long mantles, weighed down with all manner of wares. I couldn't see them clearly, so lay awhile watching until I could see more detail. The men wore fringed shirts with sashes and skullcaps. Skullcaps? Like the Seneca? Alarmed, I nudged Mëlëk.

'Look!' I whispered urgently. He wouldn't rouse, so I gave him a shove with my hand. 'Mëlëk! Natives are approaching and they aren't Lenape!'

By now they were fairly streaming toward us along the river path; one hundred or more spilling over the horizon like a huge never-ending snake. Mëlëk sleepily raised his head and peered into the distance. I swear his nut-brown skin turned cinder grey with shock.

'Make haste! We must leave!' he spat, scrambling to his feet.

My heart almost turned inside out with panic. 'Mëlëk! Who are they?'

'*Haudenosaunee!*' he gasped. 'The Haudenosaunee have come!'

THE RESCUE

One quick word from Mëlëk brought the chiefs scurrying through the trees where we crouched together, greatly alarmed by the arrival of so many Natives from a tribe who were, as far as I could tell, their masters. As the Haudenosaunee made camp near the waters of the *Lenapewihittuk*, Chief Nutimus expressed the fear in all of us, 'They have come to celebrate for they will benefit greatly from our loss. They are great in number. See! Among them are the Onondaga and the Cayuga. They plan to remain for some time for they have brought warriors, wives and slaves!'

The presence of the Haudenosaunee unsettled us to such an extent that Chief Lapowinsa suggested, rather than remain at Shackamaxon in the hope Thomas Penn might hear our complaints, we should leave in the morning and return to the settlement.

As darkness fell, a full moon shone like God's good glory, as though it had been saving itself down the ages for only this night. I slumbered but didn't sleep. The Haudenosaunee had built a huge fire and above the distant trees, I could see the glow of the flames in the night sky and hear their celebrations. Mëlëk couldn't sleep either, tossing and turning, he finally nudged me and hissed, 'Listen to them! They celebrate our woe! I *hate* them!'

He suddenly pushed back his cover, and in one noiseless movement was on his feet and running through the dark trees toward the Haudenosaunee camp.

'Mëlëk! Come back!' I hissed, but there was no point, he was already out of sight. I didn't have his stealth, so was obliged to carefully tiptoe from the fire until, clear at last, I stumbled after him. With relief, I found he had halted by the treeline, his figure a black silhouette against the distant, blazing flames.

'Aihàmtët, we are ruined!' he cried despondently. 'This injustice will never be undone!'

He was as distressed as the Haudenosaunee were triumphant. We could tell they had been drinking fermented corn because they were completely fuddled and staggering about the camp, their empty earthen pots scattered all over the grass. We should have quietly returned to our own fire, but the longer we remained, the more difficult it was to tear ourselves away from the spectacle. I'd heard so much about the Haudenosaunee they were almost mythical in my mind.

'Mëlëk, who is their chief?' I whispered.

'They are six nation so have many chief, but there is one who speak for all of them. There,' I followed the line of his finger, 'there is Canassatego. He is Speaker for the Confederacy.'

A tall, tattooed, muscular man stood near the fire, his nose ring glinting in the firelight. One glance told me he was another Kuwèmu; a breed apart from other men.

My gaze drifted toward the outer edge of the camp where a dog lay tied to a post. At least, I thought it was a dog, but as I peered through the darkness, I realised it was an emaciated slave, a woman, in ragged clothes, curled upon the ground. She was so thin I couldn't take my eyes from her, yet there was also something about her that puzzled me; her skin was pale, and her tangled hair a nut brown. I suddenly realised she was a white woman, probably the abducted wife of a settler. Whatever her previous life, she was now in a pitiful state. The great fire suddenly flared. Flames chewed the air. The woman feebly lifted her head. Firelight licked her face, and in the glow I could clearly see her sunken eyes, her hollow cheeks and dry, cracked lips – and a distinct, shrivelled, pink scar across her chin.

Ma!

It *couldn't* be her! It was impossible! She was dead! *Dead!* The breath fled from my lungs. The earth tilted. Blankness flooded over me. I crashed to the ground.

I was standing under the porch by the cabin door, fish guts at my feet. Twisted, bloody bodies lay before me in the gloom, but I felt no fear because around me floated the fragrance of yellow meadowsweet, marsh marigold and golden gorse.

'Grandma,' I whispered. 'Why am I here?'

'There's something you must see.' Her voice came from some other place, like a whispered echo through time.

'See?'

'You must look behind the door.'

Terror suddenly caught the back of my throat. 'I'm too scared. I can't bear to see what the Natives have done to Ma!'

'Don't be afeared. Look, and you will see now what you should have seen then.'

Trembling, I clasped the broken latch and peered around the edge of the door. There was nothing but shadows. Ma was not there. She was not there.

I awoke with a jolt; my skin basted in sweat and an aching lump on the side of my head. Mëlëk was kneeling beside me, urgently whispering, 'Aihàmtët! *Aihàmtët!*' I tried to sit up, but he laid a hand on my shoulder. 'Lie still. There is blood on your head.' He searched along my scalp with gentle fingers. 'The wound is small and no longer bleed. Tell me what happened?'

'I thought I saw a ghost!' I gasped.

'A *ghost*?'

'*Ma*! She's *alive*!'

'Your *mother*? I do not understand,' he exclaimed in confusion.

Despite his protestations, I struggled to my feet and pointed through the trees. 'Look – that woman – the one tied to a post.'

He squinted toward the edge of the camp, his dark eyes flashing liquid gold, mirroring the soaring flames. 'She is a white woman,' I continued excitedly, 'with chestnut hair and a scar across her chin I know well! I believed my ma was dead, but I didn't see her body. She must have been taken by the Seneca, then sold within the Haudenosaunee.' I could think of nothing but saving her. With sudden inspiration, I confidently declared, 'I'm going to rescue her – now, while it's still dark!'

Mëlëk stared at me in horror. 'If the Haudenosaunee catch you they will cut your throat!'

My bubble burst; I hadn't thought of that. Sheer exhilaration had blinded me to danger. 'Then what am I to do? I fear she is dying, and I can't bear to think she will leave this world never knowing I have found her.'

He gave no reply. Instead, he silently studied the Haudenosaunee camp with an intensity I had never seen before, as though he was steeling himself to jump from a cliff. A hundred heartbeats passed before he turned again to me. 'The warrior are drunk. They carry no weapon. There is no guard. They do not expect trouble, *but* there is no worse time to attempt a rescue than this moment. Alcohol has made them dangerous. We will wait until dawn when they sleep.'

'Brother, I alone must do this. I can't let you risk yer life.'

'Did you not risk *your* life to help Òxehëmu?'

I couldn't argue with his reasoning, especially as a droll smile now dimpled his cheeks and I realised that, despite the danger, a strike against the Haudenosaunee offered him something rare: the sweet taste of revenge.

We ran back to camp with lightning crackling in our veins. What should we tell the chiefs? Would they help? Mëlëk almost choked at that suggestion. However, to our surprise, we found they were awake and making ready for the journey home. Frowning, Chief Nutimus wagged his chin in our direction. 'Where have you been?'

I knew Mëlëk had no wish to tell outright lies to these respected men. Skirting the truth seemed the best option. 'Forgive us, we did not mean to cause concern, but could not sleep.'

'You are here now. Gather your things. We are leaving. If we remain we hear only the sound of Haudenosaunee celebration. It cannot be endured. The moon is bright. The path is waiting.'

Mëlëk threw an anxious glance toward me. 'Aihàmtët and I wish to remain and follow you tomorrow. There is something he must attend to, and I would like to go with him.'

Chief Nutimus expressed his discontent with the arrangement as the Haudenosaunee camp was only a short way through the trees but, too weary to argue, didn't press us on the matter. Taking the horses, they disappeared into the shadows, leaving us with only Samson.

The moon crept oh-so-slowly across the sky. I filled the water bottle, rolled and tied my new garments to Samson's saddle, then cooked some flatbread for Ma to eat on the journey back to the settlement. Mëlëk, meanwhile, prepared for war. Going into an enemy camp demanded the utmost readiness. He boiled the bloodroot plant as Kuwèmu had done, then painted his chest, arms and face with the crimson dye. He looked magnificent, and I caught a glimpse of the warrior I was certain he would become some day.

At last, dawn trimmed the wick. Daylight brushed the eastern horizon. My heart was racing like a rat in a barrel, but any fears I had soon turned to steadfast determination. To think in a few moments Ma would be in my arms! Kicking damp soil on the fire, I gripped Samson's reins and followed Mëlëk through the trees until we were only thirty yards from the Haudenosaunee *wikëwams*.

'Aihàmtët, now we ask the Creator for His help,' Mëlëk whispered, pausing to address the budding sunrise. Lifting his arms reverently to the sky, he chanted softly in his own speak.

I was still not on the best of terms with the Almighty, but Mëlëk's faith in the Creator never seemed to waver. The Great Spirit was as real to him as the sky and the rivers and forests, while my faith was like an old rag hung out in a gale until it was in tatters. Yet, here I was, standing only a short way from a mother I believed was dead. I couldn't make sense of it, but found myself tentatively mumbling a prayer for the first time in a year, even though I still expected my words to rise no higher than the branches above my head.

The sounds of merrymaking from the Haudenosaunee had long since fallen silent. In the centre of the deserted camp, the great fire had slumped to a glowing heap. Ma lay motionless, still tied to the post. Chirping birds piped in the rosy dawn. Geese honked on the river. Scarlet maple leaves fluttered down like three-fingered hands, but there was no human sound from the camp. We crept along the treeline toward the post. Again we crouched, watching for signs of movement among the *wikëwams* until Mëlëk was satisfied the Haudenosaunee were happily snoring.

'Aihàmtët, if they find a cut rope, they will know your mother had help to escape. You must bring the rope with you.'

I wouldn't have thought of such a thing.

Quiet as a parson at prayer, I flattened my body to the ground and began to crawl through the grass toward the post… ten yards… five yards… until at last, I was able to stretch out and wrap my fingers around Ma's thin, cold hands. She stiffened with fear. I had planned to speak calmly so she wouldn't be alarmed, but the knot in my guts suddenly uncoiled and a year's worth of sorrow came spilling over my lips in swelling sobs. 'Ma,' I whispered, 'don't be afeared. It's me – William! I've found you!'

She didn't move. Those beautiful eyes that had been so full of life lay vacant in her face. Gently, I laid a hand on her sunken cheek. 'Ma, look at me. *Look at me*! I'm not a Native. I'm William – yer *son*!'

Pulling the knife from my belt, I slit the rope binding her wrists. Her arms fell listlessly at her sides as dull, expressionless eyes continued to gaze back at me. My name meant nothing to her. She had been broken by pain and suffering until nothing of her spirit remained. She was but a shell of the woman I'd once known. Ma had gone; lost to me a second time.

I knew I mustn't linger, but neither could I tear myself away. I wasn't ready to leave her. Laying my head gently on her neck, I quietly let my grief flow warm and salty on her cold skin.

Fingertips touched my hair; the trembling caress of a hand, and a voice so faint I feared I'd imagined it, 'William?'

I pulled away. Her dull eyes were glistening.

'Yes, Ma! *Yes*!'

Joy and fear are strange companions. I was surrounded by danger, yet beaming as though I'd swallowed the sun.

From the trees, Mëlëk beckoned me to hurry. Gently, I scooped up Ma's fragile frame and, remembering to grab the rope, darted back to the cover of the trees. Mëlëk quickly wrapped his deerskin around her shivering body, but the sight of a Native made her clutch my hand.

'Don't be afeared, Ma, this is Mëlëk, my friend.' I doubt she had ever known kindness from a Native. Holding the water bottle to her lips she took a few sips, which revived her a little, then she stared at me in wonder. 'Yer *alive*! How—'

'I'll explain later, Ma. For now, we must make haste.'

Lifting her onto the saddle, I scrambled up behind her, expecting Mëlëk to swing himself up onto Samson's rump for we had to quit this place with all speed. But Mëlëk had other plans. Taking his knife, he slashed two strips of leather from the bottom of his breechcloth and hurriedly bandaged his hands. After taking a quick look around, he then leapt from the trees and ran toward the centre of the Haudenosaunee camp. My heart near jumped out of my chest with astonishment! Stopping by the glowing embers of the fire, he pulled out a small, burning log, then scurried to a *wikëwam* and placed the red-hot timber against the dry bark where the flame would take hold and reach the grass thatch covering the roof.

Back at the fire, he pulled out more burning logs and propped them against a second *wikëwam*, then a third and a fourth, until at least a dozen *wikëwams* were smouldering; the unsuspecting Haudenosaunee asleep inside believing all was well. With only a few paces between each *wikëwam*, the flames would soon devour the whole camp! Mëlëk was as clever as a fox! It was splendid revenge!

At the first sound of crackling bark, he fled back across the grass, climbed up behind me and we set off – urging Samson quickly down woody slopes and through black-water creeks until we found the path home. A mile or so later, the pungent, acrid smell of smoke floated toward us on the breeze. Stopping for a moment, we turned and stared with satisfaction at the dark, bulging clouds surging above the far treetops, and listened with relish to the distant shrieks of the Haudenosaunee as their camp burned to the ground.

WALKING AMONG THE STARS

Ma lay warm against me, her eyes round as pumpkins, studying every feature of the boy she knew in the young man before her. I didn't speak of her imprisonment or the attack at the settlement. There was nothing to be gained by those painful memories. Her time was short and those things mattered little now. Instead, I spoke of happier times and the places we loved; the bluebells along the Roe Valley, the Sperrin Mountains and the golden sands of Benone Strand. She hung on every word, but as we neared the camp and the fields I knew so well came into view, the light which had briefly flamed like a shooting star in her dark eyes suddenly faded, and I knew in my heart she had finally left this world; her beautiful brown eyes still fixed on my face.

No one paid any heed to us when we entered the camp because the tribe was consumed with news of the walk. Everywhere was noise and chatter. Arguments raged. People were shocked – frightened by the loss of land. Chief Nutimus stooped from his *wikëwam* to greet us. 'Ah, I am happy to see you have returned. These days are not without danger.' But as Mëlëk slid down from Samson's rump, the old man's face tightened like a drawstring bag. 'Why do you wear the bloodroot?' he demanded.

We both knew there was nothing for it but to tell the truth, no matter the consequences. Mëlëk took a deep breath. 'Aihàmtët believed his family had been killed, but at the Haudenosaunee camp, he recognised his mother. She had been starved and was near death. We rescued her.' He pointed briefly to the deerskin in my arms. 'She is now at peace.'

The old man's eyes bulged like a fresh-caught fish. 'You *entered* the camp of the Haudenosaunee?' At these disturbing words, a crowd began to gather.

'They did not see us,' Mëlëk assured him, 'we moved like phantoms in the mist. But I have more to tell! While the Haudenosaunee slept, I placed burning wood around their *wikëwams*. They will think the woman escaped and punished them with fire! Their camp has been devoured by flames!' He suddenly turned toward the tribe and cried, 'Behold! Mëlëk of the Lenape has destroyed the camp of the Haudenosaunee!'

The chief's face washed bone white. '*You burned down their camp?*'

There was horrified silence. All eyes fell on Mëlëk. Would he be punished or praised? Had it been a wise thing to destroy the enemy camp, or a terrible error of judgement? The chief's brown belly suddenly began to bob against his breechcloth. His saggy neck wobbled like a turkey wattle. He threw back his head and gave a resounding guffaw of laughter. 'Burned down the camp of the Haudenosaunee! How I wish I had witnessed the sight!'

His delight was infectious. Around us, folk began to chatter like starlings, marvelling at Mëlëk's cunning.

'Forgive us, Aihàmtët,' sighed Chief Nutimus at last, 'we are a broken nation and take comfort where we can. Your heart is sad and for that we are sorry. Mëlëk tells me you wish to bury your mother on this land. Take her to the high ground above the river. You may bury her there.'

Thanking him, I left Mëlëk to soak in praise while I carried Ma to the bank above the river where spring always left a carpet of bluebells in her wake. Placing her body on a bed of dry, autumn leaves, I began stabbing at the earth with my knife, scrabbling up worms and stones, so occupied I heard no other sound.

'Brother, if you will permit it, these women wish to prepare your mother for burial.'

I looked up to see Mëlëk. He carried a large buck's antler, while behind him, Mèmèkas and Nipën stood silently by the edge of the path. That anyone should offer to wash Ma's body robbed me of words. It was a kindness I hadn't expected and I could only nod gratefully in reply.

Gently lifting the deerskin, the women carried the precious load back to camp while Mëlëk split the hard earth with the antler. As the soil crumbled, I plunged my hands into the loose, damp clay and heaped it to one side until, satisfied at last with the depth, Mëlëk briefly laid a hand on my shoulder and departed, walking back to camp through the trees. He never stuck to the path.

I sat for a long time by the shallow inlet that pooled beneath the high ground. Brook trout were spawning in the clear water; their scarlet scales reflecting the blood-red sun as it dipped behind the hills leaving a quiet dusk. Swaying branches above the grave whispered their own soft lullaby, while a small beetle crawled from beneath a fallen leaf and busied itself beside my fingers; its shiny black shell like a tiny coffin on legs.

Something in the distance caught my attention. The path from the camp – a curved finger of hard-trodden soil – was twinkling as though the stars had tumbled to earth. Climbing back up the bank for a better view, I saw hundreds of lights approaching. A large procession, carrying a sea of flaming torches and singing to the solemn beat of a drum, was swaying toward me along the path.

At the head walked Mèmèkas, Nipën and Mëlëk carrying Ma on a wooden frame. The woman I knew only in rags had gone. In her place lay a figure clothed in a long, white, leather tunic. Her hair had been washed and plaited and a beaded band, with three turkey feathers perched on one side, crowned her head. A pendant of polished stone hung about her neck and in her right hand lay three of the arrows I had made myself from young willow branches.

Somehow, I succeeded in holding back the flood of salty water pricking my eyes. I knew this kindness was in gratitude for my part in saving Kuwèmu's life, although their real thanks had always been to the Great Spirit. No individual was above *kètanëtuwit*. They believed it was He who had brought me to this place as I alone had the knowledge they needed. Perhaps they were right.

Mëlëk lined the grave with dry bark, then Ma's body was placed in a sitting position as though she was simply sleeping. Blankets, skins, pots, sewing needles, knives, and food for the journey to the next world were then placed around her body. Never had a poor Irish woman been buried in such splendour, and I thanked them all for their generosity and compassion.

When the grave was finally covered, four flaming torches were thrust into the ground; one at each corner of her resting place, their golden halos casting shadows over the dark banks. I could scarce believe I'd spoken to Ma one last time. It seemed a miracle to me now, a second chance. I had longed for such a moment, yet believed it impossible, and although the ways of the Almighty still remained a mystery to me, He and I made a truce that night. I made my peace with Him. My battle was finished.

Leaving behind the steady chirping of night crickets, I walked back along the path toward the hum of Lenape voices. The chiefs were waiting; I had a letter to write. Above me, a vast, starry swirl trekked across the heavens – the Milky Way, or *opitëmakàn* as the Lenape called it – the white road to the next world. Somewhere up there, Ma was walking among the stars.

THE PARTING

I crept out early. Crimson streaks stretched across the sky like a sliced, red apple waiting for anyone who could reach it, but there would never again be a dawn for me in this place. On this morning of mornings, I untethered Samson and led him along by the river for the last time. I knew every shrub and tree, every rock and curve of the path. The canoes lay in a row like open cockle shells, each hard honed from a solid tree, and in the distance, the dark-ridged trunks of the black walnut trees stretched toward the sky. The forest beyond had already begun its slow closing down to sleep, the hunting paths I knew so well now hidden under a patchwork of scarlet and yellow leaves. The land of the Lenape would go on without me. The seasons would pass, the snows would come and the red-tail hawks would continue to soar, but I would not be there to witness it.

Stopping by the bend in the river, I laid my face against Samson's warm head and breathed in the familiar smell of his chestnut coat. In truth, I knew not what would become of my beloved horse now I was departing for Ireland. I dearly wanted to give him to Mëlëk because I knew he would attend well to him, but it would leave me with a problem: how would I reach Philadelphia in time for the sailing if I didn't have a horse? Samson snorted and gave a quick shake of his head, chasing away a few early flies, then thrust his whiskered muzzle into my hand, searching for the cornbread I always carried for him.

'Do you remember the night we slept in the woods, boy?' He pricked up his ears and steadied his dark, liquid eyes on me. 'You saved my life in those early days. I dare not think what might have become of me, but for yer company.' He seemed to sense this was something different because he suddenly nuzzled into my shoulder. I threw my arms around his neck and held on tight, trying to burn into my mind his smell, his size, his strength. There would never be another horse for me like Samson.

'Aihàmtët!' Mëlëk ambled toward me through the trees. He never stuck to the path. 'It is time. We must depart for Philadelphia!'

I knew he was eager to come with me, but I didn't want him to be caught returning alone in the forest – the Haudenosaunee were still a danger. I also knew he wouldn't be happy with my decision.

'Mëlëk, I journey alone today,' I told him, hesitantly.

His brown eyes crimped at the edges. 'But – can I not go with you?'

'Forgive me, but I won't change my mind. A lone Lenape would be easy prey for the Haudenosaunee. They will be skulking around the forests searching for bark and saplings for new dwellings. It could be fatal to come upon them. I'll be in the clothes of a white man so they won't care tuppence for me.' I raised my hands against his protests. 'Please understand, I must know you are safe with yer people. Accompany me a short way to the dogwood tree?' It wasn't what he wished, but he could see the sense of it.

Hunkering down, he scratched around in the dirt for a pebble, then skimmed the smooth, pale stone across the river. It jumped four times. Without taking his eyes from the spreading rings of water, he asked, 'Aihàmtët, what will become of Samson?'

I sighed. 'I'll be obliged to barter him for as much as possible in Philadelphia.'

'Can he not remain with me?'

'How shall I journey to Philadelphia without him?'

'Ah!' He gave that mischievous grin already etched on my memory. 'Take one of our horse – take Opim to Philadelphia and give him away before you leave.'

'Opim!' I scoffed. 'That old nag? He might drop dead on the journey!' I wore my smile like a shield, hoping it would hold back the advancing sorrow a little longer.

Eventually, we settled on a different horse: Sasapis, a grey mare that belonged to Òpalanie.

'Yer da will not be angry?'

He shook his head. 'Not if we keep Samson.'

So that was that. Samson would remain for the rest of his days with Mëlëk, and my heart sang at the thought of it.

The camp had come to life. Fires flamed as the daily tasks began, but I couldn't tarry. Captain Liston was sailing on the evening tide and those new clothes of mine were waiting. As we headed toward the *wikëwam*, a sudden quiver of expectation ran through the camp. Kuwèmu and the warriors had been sighted. Moments later they appeared, jubilant, shrieking with excitement. I recognised only one word: *manukòn*. It was the word for 'scalp'.

Kuwèmu strode amongst his people like a god; a hard-edged glint of triumph penetrating his black eyes as the tribe stood silent as a church waiting to hear of his bravery. They were not disappointed. I have never heard a man speak with such authority and purpose.

'Edward Marshall has lived his life in terror since the day of the hurry walk! He lies at night with a weapon in his hand! He has boarded his doors knowing he is loathed by the Lenape, and that someday we will seek revenge!' He held high a bloody mound of flesh. Strands of long, neatly plaited dark hair swayed from what looked like a grisly tangle of blackberries. I caught my breath as the memory of Lizzy's scalping swam before my eyes. Parading the scraggy skin around the cheering crowd, he growled, 'As he has taken from us the land we love – so we have taken from him the woman *he* loves – his wife!'

Part of me revolted at such cruelty. Kuwèmu had a savagery which unnerved me, but also made me grateful such men existed. I understood why he'd been made war-chief. He was not only brave, but ferocious in his pursuit of justice for his people. He was a natural killer. When it came to protecting the tribe, he had no equal.

Yet I also knew the Lenape would be called savages for this act, when the real savages wore waistcoats. They hid behind fine clothes so we thought them decent. They were schooled so we thought them honest. Their disguise was complete.

When Kuwèmu heard of Mëlëk's exploits at the Haudenosaunee camp, that mighty man paid a visit to our *wikëwam*. I was wriggling into my new garments when he arrived, and he gave only a quick nod in my direction before sitting beside Mëlëk, and soon they were deep in conversation.

I felt out of place, my clothes like a wall between us. I was no longer part of their world but a white boy again in shirt, breeches, leggings and boots. I hated the clothes. I felt shackled by them, and the leggings were already itchy, but more than that, I hated what they represented. Men like Penn and Eastburn wore such garments. I had no desire to be associated with them and would have happily continued in my Native clothes, but I knew Captain Liston wouldn't allow me aboard in the garments of 'a savage'.

When Kuwèmu finally departed, I placed my breechcloth, prayer stick, fowler, Bible, Ma's old pot and my moccasins inside an old hemp sack and tied it with bark fibre to keep the precious items safe. Tucking my knife and axe into Da's belt as I had that first day after the attack, I lifted my coat, bow and quiver, threw back the deerskin flap and stepped outside to find Nipën, Òpalanie and all the young'uns waiting for me. A lump the size of the moon rose in my throat. I laid my bundle on the ground, determined to say farewell without disgracing myself by weeping like a bairn.

'Wanìshi Nipën. Wanìshi Òpalanie. I will never forget...' But that damn moon wouldn't budge, and worse, morning dew had now somehow filled my eyes. With one stride, Nipën's sunshine smile drew me into her arms, and she held me as she always had – as though I belonged to her. Òpalanie handed me a deerskin. He was a good man, and I knew he wished me well, but I also knew that for both him and Kuwèmu, my time in the camp was no more than a passing breath of wind.

A small hand tugged at my shirt; Këntke was chuckling at my new garments, so it seemed as good a time as any to hoist him over my shoulder. I spun like a wheel as he shrieked with pleasure until, afeared he might vomit down my clean shirt, I lowered him into my arms and hugged his little, warm, brown body; his skin still steeped in baby scent.

Sënihële daringly wiggled a loose front tooth at me, so I grabbed him and held him upside down by his ankles until he begged for mercy. Tiyas watched without expression. I reckoned that was the best I could hope for from him, but to my surprise, he silently lifted the rabbit skin pouch from around his neck and, placing it over my head, murmured, 'Nëwitëntihëna. Kwëlaha ktëki.'

'He say you are now his brother and he wish you to return,' Mëlëk explained with a smile.

I hadn't realised Tiyas saw me as a brother. In truth, I hadn't given a single thought to him because I believed he barely tolerated my presence within the camp. He hadn't spoken one word to me, yet now had the look of a young dog hoping for scraps. I laid a comforting hand on his shoulder, and with the same word he had used, nëwitëntihëna, which meant 'we are brothers', he was admitted into the world Mëlëk and I shared. Delight creased his cheeks, and not for the first time I wished I had my own brother beside me.

Òxehëmu threw her arms tightly around my waist. Kissing the top of her head, I whispered, 'Farewell, Moonlight.' She frowned. I explained in simple terms: 'Òxehëmu – Moonlight.'

'Mun-leet,' she repeated, giggling bashfully. I was going to miss that impish grin.

The chosen horse, Sasapis, seemed calm enough until I tried to saddle her, then she bucked like a bellyache. In truth, the saddle was not worth the effort because the stitching had frayed and the leather had split. It was fit for nothing but burning. I heaved it to Mëlëk with a grin. 'Here – destroyer of *wikëwams*. You have a natural ability for burning things.' Why did we laugh with such ease? Perhaps it was the only thing that prevented us from weeping.

Mëlëk swung himself up onto Samson. I slung my bow and quiver over my shoulder and climbed onto Sasapis, resting the deerskin, hemp sack and my fur coat over her mane. I was riding without a saddle. It wasn't the first time, although I reckoned it would probably be the last time. As we trotted through the settlement, many of the women waved and some of the children ran alongside until we left the camp. I didn't expect Kuwèmu to bid me farewell. It was a privilege just to have been acquainted with such a man.

Trotting along the wide, well-worn path toward Philadelphia, I voiced my fears for the Lenape, 'What will become of yer tribe now such a large amount of land has been lost?'

'We will continue to bring our complaint before Thomas Penn, but I do not believe he will hear our grievance. He give no thought to us. We are but a stone in his shoe.' Avoiding my eyes, Mëlëk suddenly looked embarrassed. 'Aihàmtët, there is something I must tell you. I did not save you from the riverbank. I wanted you to die.

It was my father and Këkëlëksu who saved you. I did not want a white boy in our camp.' He lifted his dark-eyed gaze. 'But the Great Spirit spoke to me – "You must learn, Mëlëk of the Lenape! I will teach you! See! You and the white boy are like the wolf and dog, but you will not become enemy! You will always be friend!"'

'Mëlëk, don't feel ashamed,' I consoled. 'I understand why you hate white men; they have taken yer land. I hate Natives because they took my kin. We both know what it is to suffer at the hands of cruel men. Some wear breechcloths and some wear waistcoats, but evil is the same in any 'guise because it lives in a man's soul. My grandma taught me that, and she should know because she can see the darkness in people.'

We halted under the deep-red dogwood leaves. It was no great distance from the camp, but ten miles wouldn't have been far enough because neither of us wished to say farewell.

'I got the letter tucked in my breeches.' I patted my pocket to make sure it was safe. 'I promise I will do all I can to put it into the hands of the sovereign.'

'I know you will not fail us, brother.'

'Mëlëk, a reverend once told me God works in mysterious ways. I can't say even now if I understand, but of one thing I'm certain, I am glad we met. I will never forget you, my friend.'

Reaching across to me, he folded his brown fingers above my wrist. I curled my hand tightly around his forearm in the same way. It was a good hold. A strong hold. A hold to last a lifetime.

'I will carry you in my heart and ask the Great Spirit to watch over you, Aihàmtët. I will call your name to the wind. Maybe someday, it will carry my voice across the ocean and you will hear me.'

For a moment we held steady as I drank in the sound of his voice and the wildness of his spirit. Mëlëk would now be added to the list of people I would never again set eyes on for the rest of my life, and the hole it left inside me was darker than the blackest night. If I had lived with the Lenape above twenty years, I still would not have mastered their speak as Mëlëk had mastered English. His skill and intelligence far outweighed mine, and I was proud to call him my brother.

Turning Sasapis toward Philadelphia, I gave the horse a good kick on the flank. 'Mèchi ntalëmska!' I called over my shoulder. I wanted my last words to Mëlëk to be in his own language. I'd practised for days, certain the meaning was, 'I am leaving now'.

A throaty chuckle that was silver to my soul echoed back to me, 'You say I have the face of an elk!' he teased.

I raised an arm, but didn't turn around because my heart was too near splintering. As the bowels of the forest drew me in, and the trees began to thicken, I finally halted and glanced backward. The camp lay in the distance. I could hear the faint laughter of children playing by the river and see smoke rising from the fires. Mëlëk, almost home, raised an arm to the sky and called, 'Farewell, my friend! Farewell, William Baxter of Limavady!'

Then he melted among the wikëwams like pine sap under a summer sun.

THE SOVEREIGN OF BÉAL FEIRSTE

On a watery December morning, the *Mary* finally sailed past Carrickfergus then on through the lough toward Béal Feirste. Under strands of silver sleet, traders along the banks hawed on their hands and hugged their coats like long-lost sweethearts. Lime-washed cottages crouched against the cold, their stone walls curiously unfamiliar after the *wikëwams* and wooden cabins of Penn's country.

'What river is this, Scuttle-Butt?' I called up toward the rigging, where he must have been near frozen to a statue.

'The River Lagan!' he shouted down to me.

I gazed across the water at my first view of Béal Feirste and the snow-covered, forested hills that girdled the town. It was certainly not as grand as Philadelphia, nor numbered as many fine buildings. In truth, it was low-lying and looked a mite damp to me.

'Hard a starboard!' ordered Captain Liston.

The ship glided into a narrow channel. 'Scuttle-Butt!' I cried. 'Will we not scrape the sides?'

'We ain't no forty-gun man-o'-war, Master Baxter!' he laughed. 'This 'ere channel is the Farset River. It's narrow, but don't you fret boy, we ain't gonna get trammelled!'

We were suddenly in the heart of the town. Stone houses and shops bordered each bank. Folk scurried around in the cold, unloading cargo, hauling sacks of flour and sugar, while merchants engaged in hurried discussions on the quayside. When the bowline was secure, Captain Liston, a large ledger under one arm, stepped across the gangplank and headed in the direction of the customs house. I shook hands with Scuttle-Butt and thanked him. I would miss the old sailor.

Wrapped warmly in my coat, I slung my bow and quiver over my shoulder, grabbed the hemp sack carrying all my precious belongings, and stepped at last onto Irish soil. In truth, I would gladly have knelt and kissed that dear land, except dogs and pigs were plentiful about the street, so I thought twice about laying my lips to the ground.

Nearby, a woman was selling hot chestnuts. Hugging a grey shawl tightly around her head and shoulders, she wiped a hand across her red, raw nose and coughed as though she had rusty lungs; her misty breath fleeing like a phantom in the early light. I was gut-foundered and in dire need of a hot meal, but hadn't so much as one farthing in my pocket.

'Good day, madam. May I stand awhile by yer fire?'

'Indeed you may, young sir, there is no charge for the warmth.' She looked admiringly at my coat. 'That's a fine winter coat you got there.'

'It was made by a friend in the New World. I've newly arrived across the flood.'

'Then you'll be near starved! Those ships are quick to take yer money for passage but haven't a care if you starve to death on the journey! Here,' she fussed, 'take off yer glove and put a few of these inside you.'

'Madam,' I feebly protested, 'I got nothing for payment.'

'Ah, houl yer wheest, now! I'll have none of that! It's the blessed season of giving, and you are rightly welcome!'

Pulling off my gloves, I held out a cupped hand. The woman dropped six warm chestnuts into my palm, the shells already cracked for peeling. Their smoky taste lay on my tongue long after they had slipped down my throat and warmed my belly.

'May I beg a question, madam?'

She wiped her nose on the back of her hand, sniffed like a hog, swallowed a great gob of something and replied, 'I'll answer if I can, lad.'

'Does the sovereign live here in the town?'

'Indeed he does, but he'll not have his fat frame outside on a day like this! His name is Margetson Saunders, and you'll find him at the market house or the corporation church on Sunday.'

'Where is the market house? Is it some distance?'

'Not at all, laddie!' She pointed further along the street. 'It's there at the corner of High Street and Corn Market. You'll find it with ease; it's a red brick building with a tower and a clock. It also serves as the courthouse.' She gave a devilish grin. 'If the sovereign is there, he'll be deciding which poor wretch to hang!'

'I'm much obliged to you, madam, and grateful for the chestnuts. Thank you for yer kindness.' But as I made to leave she laid a hand on my arm.

'Might I ask where you live?'

'My home is Newtown-Limavady. I begin my journey this day up through the Glens of Antrim.'

'Don't go through those hills, young sir!' she warned. 'There are robbers and villains hiding there!'

I shrugged. 'It's of no matter because I got no money.'

'That may be, but they will take yer hunting bow and that coat from yer back! Take the path by the coast!' she insisted.

I decided to heed her advice, even though I felt equal to any robber. In truth, I would like to see anyone try to relieve me of my possessions because I reckoned there wasn't another lad in the whole of Ireland who could fight like me. I had been schooled in combat by the very best – a war-chief of the Lenape tribe.

Bidding her farewell, I made haste and found the Market House with ease. Pushing open the heavy wooden door, I stepped into a large, warm, noisy room overflowing with merchants and traders, all bartering the price of baccy, sugar, cotton and other goods – shaking hands or shaking heads at the expense. Two high-backed wooden benches sat either side of a blazing fire, while on a table by the door lay several quills, a pot of ink, leaves of parchment, a pile of books and a well-fingered sheet of the *Belfast Newsletter and General Advertiser*. I confess I found it all most interesting, but I didn't see anyone who looked as though they might be the sovereign because surely that gentleman would be dressed in the best finery coppers could buy.

The merchants paid little heed to me, so I crossed to the dark wooden stairs and made my way up to a small landing on the first floor where a solid oak door prevented my going any further. I waited, trying to decide if I should knock because I had no wish to disturb the court and get a scolding for my efforts. Holding my breath, I listened at the door, but heard no sound. I glanced over the stair rail to the room below, wondering if I should ask someone if the court was in session, when suddenly, with a loud creak, the door swung open and a gentleman with a 'fat frame' stared at me. His garments were those of a man of position: embroidered waistcoat, knee-length coat, matching breeches, white stockings and silver buckles on his shiny black shoes. Finding me blocking his descent, he enquired as to my business. Respectfully, I pulled off my gloves.

'Good day, sir. I'm in search of Margetson Saunders, the Sovereign of Béal Feirste.'

He eyed me with haughty indifference. 'I am the sovereign. What is the nature of your business?'

He didn't offer his hand, so I grabbed it anyway and gave a mighty shake. 'I'm rightly glad to make yer acquaintance, sir! My name is William Baxter, and I carry a letter of great importance from the Lenni Lenape tribe of Penn's country for the King of England!'

'A letter? For His Majesty?' He gave a short grunt. 'From a tribe of savages!'

His mocking unnerved me, but I continued, 'Sir, you may be in a position to carry the letter to the king, or know someone trustworthy who may be engaged for that purpose? It is of the utmost importance.'

Paying little heed to my words, he drew a pocket watch from his waistcoat and studied the gold-rimmed face. 'I am a busy man, young sir, and have little time for blabber!'

Dismayed, I steadied myself. I daresay he was a busy man, but I had journeyed across an entire ocean to present him with the letter and would not be easily swayed from the task!

'Sir, if I may have a little of yer time,' I pleaded.

He sighed like a cross old woman who had lost her best cooking pot. 'Oh, very well. Come where it is warm, but I warn you, I can spare but a brief moment!'

We descended the stairs and pushed our way through the noisy crowd to the fire, where he lifted his coat-tails and turned his fat rump toward the warmth.

'Lay your belongings on the settle, boy,' he ordered. I placed my bow, quiver and sack on one of the high-backed benches. 'Now, explain yourself and be quick about it.'

I was obliged to speak loudly due to the din in the room, and hoped I didn't sound impolite. 'Sir, the Lenape Natives have been cheated out of their lands by Governor Thomas Penn.'

'Cheated by Penn? Never! Why, I have always found Governor Penn a most honest and amiable fellow.'

Honest? Amiable? Was the man in jest? 'Sir, I can assure you that Governor Penn has defrauded the Lenape Natives!'

He gave me a quizzical look. 'How, boy? How has he defrauded the savages?'

This man obviously knew nothing of that wild country. How could I make him understand? I stumbled into explanation, 'An amount of land was to be measured by means of a walk, but Governor Penn hired skilled runners who covered twice the expected distance. Then his surveyor Eastburn—'

'What nonsense is this about a walk? What care I for a "walk"?!' he stated impatiently.

Before I could reply, a loud handbell rang, and merchants and traders alike scooped up their charts and drifted toward the door. Margetson Saunders also made ready to leave, so I quickly pulled the letter from my pocket, as now might be my only opportunity to deliver it into his hand. I had addressed it to *His Gracious Majesty King George II of England*, and Chief Nutimus had sealed it with pine sap. For the briefest moment I ran my finger over the knob of dry gum and wished those four chiefs were standing with me now, weapons in hand, and this foolish fop of a sovereign on the floor begging for his life!

'Sir, if I may be so bold, I humbly beg you to take this letter and see it reaches the king!' I pleaded a final time.

His mouth inched at the corners. It wasn't a true smile because his eyes remained fixed with contempt, yet I found myself drawn in by the hope he had truly heard my grievance.

'Very well, young man, I will endeavour to carry out your wishes.' And with a fat finger and thumb, he daintily plucked the letter from my hand.

'You have my most grateful thanks, sir!' I was barely able to believe I'd accomplished the task, and was so overcome with relief and good cheer I bowed my way out of that room as though *he* was the King of England! I could return to Limavady now with a light heart, my duty discharged. He would give the letter to the king, and Thomas Penn would be ordered to return the Lenape land!

Outside it was beginning to snow. I pulled up my hood and bent to lift my bow – *what a dunce you are*, I thought to myself – my belongings still lay on the wooden settle in the market house. I was in danger of forgetting my head with happiness! Pushing open the door, I was just in time to see the flick of Margetson Saunders' wrist. It took no more than that to send the letter into the blazing flames.

'No!' I leapt forward, but the heat had instantly devoured the paper. Whirling around, I exploded with fury. 'That letter was their only hope of justice! You shall pay for this wickedness!'

'Do you *threaten* me, boy?' He advanced toward me, glowering, unrepentant, his voice steady and menacing. 'Did you truly believe the King of England would be concerned with the grievances of savages? That land was given to Thomas Penn's father with no thought of its inhabitants, why would we now be concerned with their plight? England will have that land, by God it will, and no letter from a tribe of savages will prevent it!'

The fop had disappeared, and in his place was this swine – another Thomas Penn! I had been so naïve, so foolish and trusting! If he had only realised how close he came to being killed because I could have drawn my knife and slit his throat in an instant! Brushing past me, he flung open the door and disappeared in a flurry of tailcoat leaving me reeling; staggered by his callousness. I sat down hard on the settle. The Lenape would be waiting, hoping for news from the great King of England. Mëlëk would never know of my efforts, and only the passage of years would tell I had failed.

I stared numbly into the fire until an elderly man pushed open the door and informed me I must leave; the market house was to be bolted until the morrow. Wearily, I lifted my bow, quiver and sack and tramped outside to find the snow falling thick and fast, covering the streets and thatched roofs like a vast sheet of white linen.

I quit that town, happy to kick it from my heels, and trudged along the coastal path where the dark ocean lashed the rocky shore and grey gulls battled the headwind. Before me lay days of winter walking, begging for shelter and food. Heartsick with disappointment, there was only one thought that drove me on through that blinding snow: the warm, welcoming arms of my grandma.

HOME

I stood ankle-deep in snow at the bend in the road, barely able to contain my joy at the sight of Limavady. In the three years I'd been away, it hadn't changed. Thatches white as sugar-ice draped over cottage walls like the feathers of a mother hen over her chicks. Hawthorn and holly berries hung from frosted branches, while the familiar smell of burning turf rose from warm chimneys. A tangle of bare honeysuckle vine curled around the old hollow oak where I used to crouch for hours waiting for James to discover me, only to find he'd long since given up the game and taken himself home.

All was quiet. There wasn't a soul out in the shadowy twilight save a young girl, who rammed a booted foot into the iced water of a small pond for her waddling geese. She stared at me as though I hailed from another world. Indeed, she wasn't much mistaken. I had left this place a small, hungry lad of thirteen and was returning a tall young man of sixteen with a knowledge of the world few people my age possessed.

Leaving a winding snake of footprints in the snow, I trudged past the wooden punishment stocks and large wooden cross in the centre of the village, and headed down the road toward Aunt Sarah's cottage. I would first call upon my aunt as Grandma lived in an old, windowless roundhouse further along the lane.

Lamplight shone softly through the cracks in Aunt Sarah's door, falling honey-gold on the snow. The wood was flaking with age. It needed a good basting of flax oil, and it pleased me greatly to think I could now be of help to both my aunt and my grandma. I rapped on the door, ants crawling in my guts with nervous excitement because although I was much relieved to be home, I also carried the sad news of her sister's death.

From inside came the sound of clanging pots followed by the muttering of an oath; she could curse like a soldier. I braced myself for the stink-breath about to envelope me as the door swung open, but a woman, much thinner than I remembered and wearing a black shawl, black skirt and unlaced black boots, stared back at me. Or rather, one eye stared at me. The bochety eye was aimed elsewhere.

'If yer looking for scraps, I got scarce enough to feed myself!' she exclaimed, and slammed the door. This wasn't the homecoming I'd anticipated.

Again, I knocked on the peeling wood, and when she pulled the latch, I swiftly placed my foot on the doorstep and cried, 'Aunt Sarah, it's William – yer nephew, William Baxter!'

The mention of my name halted that woman in every way; she stopped moving, stopped blinking. I could almost hear the whirr and click of her brain as it chimed the unbelievable. 'Glory be! *William!* Is it yerself?'

'The very same, Aunt!'

Her face suddenly sagged like an old hemp sack. Struggling to breathe against rising tears, she flung her arms about my neck, pressing her face tightly against my chest as deep, convulsing sobs shook her whole body. I clung to her like a lost child, hiding my wet cheeks in her thick hair, no longer caring if her breath sent me reeling – I was home.

At last, she drew back and ran her rough hands over my hair and face, feeling the curves of my bones like Ma had done when I fell off the cabin roof – as though she couldn't quite believe I was still in one piece.

'Look at the length and width of you, lad!' Aunt Sarah was accustomed to measuring linen. 'I can scarce believe my eyes! Are youse all returned from across the flood?'

Filled with the sudden hope Ma and Da might be coming down the lane behind me, she started eagerly out the door, but I blocked her path with a quick sideway step and laid a hand on her shoulder. 'Aunt Sarah, I alone have returned.'

I could have told her they were all alive and happy in their new life, and that only I wanted to return to Ireland, but it seemed best to be truthful, or at least skirt the truth. Placing the Bible on her lap, I showed her the date of their deaths and said they died of a fever. I spoke not one word of the attack or the year of suffering her sister had endured at the hands of the Haudenosaunee. Those memories belonged only to me.

After some time, I lifted my coat and, begging her forgiveness for departing, explained I had a great need to see Grandma. Misfortune loves a friend. That was another of Ma's sayings, and I was about to discover the truth of it.

'But, William,' tears broke over her lashes and flooded her pale cheeks, 'yer gran is no longer in the roundhouse. She's in the churchyard.'

I stared at her in amazement. 'In this weather? How could you let her go talking to the dead when there's a foot of snow on the ground! She'll be foundered – and her coughing with the tar-lung!'

'Pay heed to me, lad,' her voice trembled like reeds in a rising wind, 'yer gran isn't talking to the dead. She lies by the boundary wall alongside them.'

The tower I had built to keep out all the misery and suffering, was suddenly breached and came crashing down, my heart lost somewhere in the rubble.

'No! *No!* It can't be! Tell me it isn't true!'

She reached for the bottle of whisky.

We two sat by the fire, each wrapped in grief, as snow drifted silently over the quiet lanes and cottages to settle on the earth that hid my grandma's sleeping soul. I should have realised she was dead. How could she have come to me if she was still alive? The living can't transport their spirit. Only those who have passed on are free to roam like seeds upon the wind.

'When did she die?' I sniffed.

'The autumn of '36, more than a year gone.'

I thought back to the settlement. I would have been harvesting the pumpkins and chopping wood. Could it be possible she died the same day as the attack knowing how much I would need her?

'Was it the tar-lung that killed her?'

She nodded. 'Her poor lungs rattled like a bag of bones.'

'Were you with her at the last?'

'Indeed I was; I never left her side. You needn't fret, William, she wasn't alone, although she lost all reason toward the end.'

'Lost her reason?' Grandma had always been in full possession of her wits.

'Aye lad, her ravings were all a jumble – I never heard the like of it! She gave me the frights with her imaginings and strange visions – bodies on the ground, painted men, and a young bird afraid to fly! "Stop yer blethering, woman!" said I, but she grabbed my hand and told me it was time for her to quit this earth, or that young bird wouldn't find the courage to leave its nest!'

The drummer in my chest dropped a stick.

'What bird?'

'I believe it was a bird of prey – a falcon.'

'A falcon?'

'No, let me think now.' She chewed a moment on her gums. 'It was a hawk.'

'A hawk?'

'Mmm,' the hum lingered. 'No, indeed now, it wasn't a hawk.' Rising, she lifted a booted foot and nudged grey ash from the edge of the hearth back toward the glow. 'Ah now, patience, William. It'll come to me.'

'Aunt Sarah, I beg you. Think!'

'Will you have a drop more?' she asked, picking up the whisky bottle from the hearth.

'Aunt Sarah!' I pleaded.

'Ah, I have it now!' Heaven be praised because at last, she wagged the finger. 'It was an *eagle!* She called the bird her Young Eagle.'

OF TYRANNY AND TRIBES

Many years have passed since my return from Philadelphia. I am now almost seventy-five years of age, thin shanked with a stooped back and lumpy finger joints. Yet still, I dwell on the past. My memories are as strong as the pull of the tide, and I scold myself often for thinking of those I left behind in the New World because it always makes me unsettled.

I built my log cabin by the River Roe just as I'd described it to Mëlëk. My carved prayer stick, hunting bow, quiver and arrows hang against the back wall, while bracelets and necklaces decorated with shells in the style of the Lenape, lie along the beams. My breechcloth rests on a shelf by the bed, and in the early hours when I can't sleep, I run my fingers over the soft leather and wonder what has become of my friend.

My failure over the letter has weighed heavily on me for almost sixty years. There have been times I thought I would drown under the burden of it. If I could have had two minutes with Mëlëk to tell him of my meeting with the sovereign, I would have slept more fitfully through the years.

When word of my adventures reached the good folk of Limavady, and indeed, the rest of Ulster, I became known as 'Indian Bill'. People came from miles to hear my tales. They arrived on foot, on carts, and some even came in fine carriages, crowding the cabin and overflowing onto the porch, such was the demand to hear of my time in the New World.

Aunt Sarah died seven years after my return. The last thing to pass her lips was a flip; the drink of her dreams. I promised to bury her with all the ingredients. Although ailing, she had attended my wedding to Grace; the best wife a man could have desired, God rest her soul. We had five bairns, all now grown and tossed like wild berries around the town, earning their keep. They are my joy.

I learned a trade and became a dry-tight cooper – making barrels to hold gunpowder, flour and other dry goods for the ocean-going ships. But I'm the only cooper in Ireland to smear a light covering of duck fat on the wooden staves so they don't burn when I bend them over the fire, and my barrels are widely admired. The merchant calls to collect them once a week, and I still had one to finish, but I slept in a chair by the fire yesterday instead – warmer on my old bones these days.

Glancing toward the door, splinters of morning blue pierced the small cracks in the planks. It was time I made a start on the day's work. Rising stiffly, I stretched my aching muscles and hobbled out onto the porch. It was going to be a grand autumn day.

I began by bringing in wood for the fire, then threw a handful of grain to Brown Bess, my one remaining chicken following a visit from the fox. I named her after the musket carried by the English soldiers as she too is slow, unreliable and looks me straight in the eye.

Placing two potatoes among the hot cinders for my evening meal, I poured a little water into my old black pot and placed it on the flames. Once a week, I allowed myself warm chocolate. It was an expense, but reminded me of Erik, and I always drank it under the porch in the morning mist.

Picking up the pincers and tongs, I had just begun work on the unfinished barrel when there was a rap at the door. Frowning, I looked toward the sound. No one ever called on me except the merchant for the barrels or my bairns, but it wasn't their day to visit. Muttering with annoyance, I shuffled across the deerskin mat and tugged the latch.

A young, freckle-tanned lad with a satchel across his chest, and golden hair that tumbled like ripe wheat around his grey eyes, stood under the porch. He gave me a wide, cheek-puckering grin. A cheery soul and no mistake, I decided.

'Good day, sir. Might I enquire if you are,' he took a letter from his satchel, turned it the right way up and read, 'William Baxter?'

'Indeed, William Baxter is my name,' I replied, perplexed.

'Then I have discovered you, at last, sir!' The lad's entire countenance bubbled. 'I have come from the post office on East Derry Hill, to bring you a letter delivered to us some three weeks since.'

'A letter?' There was not a soul of my acquaintance who could write.

He nodded enthusiastically. 'Yer letter is the first correspondence we have had from Pennsylvania!'

I snatched the door frame for support.

'It was sent from the post office at Philadelphia to New York, then by the packet ship *Halifax* to Falmouth, carried through Holyhead to Dublin, then by coach to Béal Feirste and finally by post rider to Londonderry. It has taken almost three months to arrive!'

His words bounced inside my head like loose cannonballs. 'May I see the letter?' I asked, reaching to take it.

He held it a little way beyond my outstretched hand. 'Postage must first be paid, sir. It amounts to one shilling and nine pence. Pennsylvania is a *very* long way!'

I was in such a state of panicked excitement I barely heard his words. There was only one person in the whole of Pennsylvania who knew where I lived, but he could neither read nor write and may not even be alive after all these years.

'Payment, sir?' The young man's voice dragged me back to the present.

Lifting an old tin from the shelf, I tipped what money I had onto the small, pine table and began to count; two farthings, add a penny, add sixpence... until eventually, I dropped a collection of coins into his grubby palm. He handed the letter to me with a slight bow. 'I am pleased to be of service, sir.' Then stepping from the porch back into the sunshine, he disappeared down the lane.

Closing the door, I turned the paper in my hands, feeling the folds, running my fingers over the writing and ship's stamp.

William Baxter
Newtown-Limavady
Ulster
Ireland

The paper had been sealed with pine sap. Trembling, I lowered myself onto the chair, carefully peeled away the seal and unfolded the sheet. The writing was small and filled every inch of the paper. Indeed, the author had even turned the sheet and continued along the top and sides to such an extent I had to light a candle and use my eyeglass for ease of reading, searching for the beginning among the hodgepodge of words.

24th June 1796

Aihàmtët,

I embrace you, my dear friend and brother.

Should this letter find you alive and in good health, I send my warmest greetings. A reverend of your Christian faith has told me it is now possible to send news across the ocean, and as I have spoken often of my white brother, he has kindly offered to write my words.

In hope this letter reaches you, I will endeavour to relate some of what has occurred since your parting. I know you will not have forgotten the walk and the injustice we suffered, but you will be unaware of our disgrace at the hands of the Haudenosaunee. For five years we fought our case, writing again to the British Crown, but all correspondence went mysteriously astray. Do not blame yourself if the letter you carried met with no success. I am certain you tried your utmost on our behalf.

Our only option was to beg help from the Haudenosaunee, and so we presented ourselves with gifts to Canassatego. What fools we were! He admonished us, saying we were an unruly people and he was weary with our complaints and should shake us by our hair for our insolence! He demanded to know by what right we had entered into negotiations with Thomas Penn without permission, reminding us we had been conquered by them long ago and they had made women of us and women cannot sell land! We were ordered to leave our ancestral lands and never return. Such humiliation! Never had we been so dishonoured and shamed.

We journeyed to the Wyoming Valley and remained there for some years, during which time you will be sad to hear that beautiful Oxehëmu was murdered by settlers as she gathered berries; she had strayed onto their land. We repaid them by taking their scalps.

You will also be distressed to know Tiyas, Sënihële and our great war-chief Kuwèmu were killed fighting with the French against the English. We sided with the French in revenge for the deceit of Thomas Penn.

Once again we were forced west, settlers always on our heels. A great revolution swept the land, and I cannot find the words to tell you of the dread massacre that befell some of our tribe at a place called Gnadenhutten. We continued west. Two years ago we joined other tribes and fought against the American soldiers. There had been a great storm, and we fought bravely among forests of fallen timbers, believing it would be an advantage against men on horseback, but we were defeated and much tribal land was lost.

I fight no more. I am too old. Following the battle, my heart cried out for my homeland. I turned my face east and together with Këntke, his family and my own two dear daughters, I walked home. The journey took many months, but I am again in the land of my birth, the land we both knew, although it is not as I remember for we are surrounded by many fences and boundaries. The forests have been felled to allow the planting of crops, so there is little hunting, but thankfully the rivers still give us fish and we live quietly with a small number of other Lenape.

My father and mother have long since flown this world. Chief Nutimus lived over one hundred years. He is still greatly missed. Were you ever wed, Aihàmtët? Do you have children? I am told the paper will hold few more words. The Reverend Nathan Grier will take this correspondence to Philadelphia. If possible, send word to the Forks of the Brandywine Presbyterian Church, Pennsylvania. Reverend Grier will endeavour to carry your words to me.

I bid you farewell, dear brother. I will look for your letter every day. Tell me you have not forgotten me.

Your devoted brother,
Mëlëk.

The paper soaked up my joy as though I'd read it in the rain. A lifetime of wondering settled in the sheet of words crumpled between my fingers.

'Forgotten you, my friend?' I choked. '*Never*! I will write this very day and tell you of my life and all my news!' At last, I could make known to him my meeting with that ruthless sovereign at Béal Feirste! But what bittersweet tidings. Oxehëmu, Tiyas and Sënihële, dead. Kuwèmu slaughtered. I laid the precious letter on the table and smoothed out the creases. I needed paper, quill and ink, but such items weren't sold in Limavady as few here could read or write. A journey to Londonderry was required and I would leave this very moment. Suddenly there was urgency; every nerve and sinew in my body thrilled with excitement.

Counting what money remained in my tin, I realised I would need more than a few pennies for ink alone. I looked around the cabin. What could I sell? Unhooking the beaded necklaces from the beams, I laid them gently in my satchel; they would fetch a good price. Now, I would need some food with me for the journey. Scraping the cinders from the hot potatoes, I wrapped them in a rag of linen, placed them with the necklaces, and flung on my coat; the fur still thick and warm after sixty years. Derry was almost twenty miles away, but there would be carts trundling toward the town and I could hop on for a ride. Tugging the latch behind me, I stepped eagerly along the lane toward the bridge, as the chatter of women on their way to market echoed through the streets. On the outskirts of the town a milkmaid was about her work; the gentle *swish, swish* of milk from the udder like a whisper on the breeze. In a flat field, two sturdy garron puffed clouds of steaming breath as they pulled a plough in the brume, their young, red-cheeked master stumbling behind, gripping the plough handles with raw, chapped hands. Below the wooden bridge that spanned the clear waters of the Roe, shiny black elderberries shrouded the banks in plump bunches, shading salmon returning to spawn.

The road to Derry lay before me in the sun. With a fire of hope in my belly, I began to run – as much as a giddy old man of my age *can* run. In that far-away land, where the wind wanders through the sassafras trees, and *sëpi shukël* is gathered when the snows melt, and the rivers ripple in the spring with shad, Mëlëk was waiting.

HISTORICAL NOTE

Young Eagle Rising is a work of fiction. While I have included various historical characters, the book is not intended to be a rigorous work of historical fact and should not be used for historical reference.

APPENDIX

Several years before 1735, a ship named the *Mary Galley* sailed under Captain Liston with passengers from Londonderry to Philadelphia. I used this information when placing William and his family on-board the *Mary*.

The first coffee house in Philadelphia opened its doors around 1703 on the east side of Front Street and was known as *Ye Coffee House*. A later coffee house opened in 1754, *The London Coffee House*.

Benjamin Franklin became one of America's Founding Fathers. His signature is on the Declaration of Independence. When William chanced to meet him, Franklin would have been about 30 years of age and already publishing the *Pennsylvania Gazette*.

Derry Church, Pennsylvania, was founded in 1729. William Bertram, native of Scotland, became the reverend there in 1732.

George Gibson's tavern in King Street, Lancaster (previously known as Hickory Town), was called *The Hickory Tree Tavern* as there had been a large hickory tree nearby that was a known meeting place for Natives.

Peter (Pierre) Bazaillon was born in 1662 in France. One of five brothers, he came to New France to trade with the Natives. He had a long and interesting life and died in July 1742, aged 80 years, leaving large estates in the Susquehanna Valley to his widow.

Of the five remaining De Burt children who fled to Virginia, one son, Christopher, returned to his father's land in 1740 with his wife and young son. He was killed and scalped by Natives in 1757.

The Native Americans of Nova Scotia used a plant known as a pitcher plant to cure smallpox: *Sarracenia purpurea*. Science has proved it suppresses the virus.

The 'walk', which resulted in the Lenape (also known as the Delaware tribe) losing one thousand two hundred square miles, is today known as The Walking Purchase. Yeates died three days after the walk, and Jennings suffered pain for the rest of his life. In 1756, Edward Marshall's home was attacked and his wife abducted and killed by Natives. In 1757 his son was also killed.

In August 1794 the Battle of Fallen Timbers was fought between the forces of General Wayne and a union of tribes including the Mayaimi (Chief Little Turtle), Shawnees (Chief Blue Jacket) and Lenape (Chief Buckongahelas).

Béal Feirste was the Irish Gaelic name for what became Belfast. The name in Ulster-Scots is Bilfawst.

The first post office in Londonderry was in Thom's Tavern, East Derry Hill, and opened in 1795.

The packet ship *Halifax* sailed between America and Falmouth under Captain Stanhope. Records show it left Falmouth on 24th

June 1796 and arrived in Halifax (Nova Scotia) on 6th August. From Halifax it sailed to New York, arriving the 20th August. It then left New York on 8th September, finally arriving again at Falmouth on 19th October 1796.

To discover the meaning of the Native American names and words in the book, search www.talk-lenape.org/

For writing and publishing news, or
recommendations of new titles to read,
sign up to the Book Guild newsletter: